A **MISSIO** PLAYBOOK

MADE FOR MORE

Being Disciples. Making Disciples.

Kent Ingle and Steve Saccone

Published by Missio Publishing
Made For More
Copyright © 2023 Kent Ingle and Steve Saccone

This title is also available as an ebook. Visit: missiopublishing.com

For more info or to find out about bulk discounts:
info@missiopublishing.com

ISBN 978-1-7328063-3-7

All scripture quotations, unless otherwise indicated, are taken from the Holy Bible, New International Version®, NIV®. Copyright ©1973, 1978, 1984, 2011 by Biblica, Inc.™ Used by permission of Zondervan. All rights reserved worldwide. www.zondervan.com The "NIV" and "New International Version" are trademarks registered in the United States Patent and Trademark Office by Biblica, Inc.™

Scripture quotations from THE MESSAGE. Copyright © by Eugene H. Peterson 1993, 1994, 1995, 1996, 2000, 2001, 2002. Used by permission of NavPress Publishing Group.

Scripture quotations marked (NLT) are taken from the Holy Bible, New Living Translation, copyright © 1996, 2004, 2007 by Tyndale House Foundation. Used by permission of Tyndale House Publishers, Inc., Carol Stream, Illinois 60188.

Printed in Canada.

All rights reserved. No part of this publication may be reproduced, stored in a retrieval system, or transmitted in any form or by any means, except for brief quotations in printed reviews, without the prior permission of the publisher.

CONTENTS

An Untold Story	Introduction	4
An Unusual Choice	Week 1	18
An Unwavering Connection	Week 2	52
An Uncommon Pursuit	Week 3	84
An Unexpected Calling	Week 4	108
An Unselfish Heart	Week 5	142
An Unstoppable Mission	Week 6	176
An Unscripted Future	Conclusion	210

INTRODUCTION

AN UNTOLD STORY

God has a dream for your life! You have a unique purpose and a divine destiny.

There's a remarkable metaphor in nature that displays what we believe God desires to do in and through your life. There is a small insect that starts as an egg. After a few days, a caterpillar emerges out of that egg. Then, what does this tiny caterpillar want to do? Eat.

If you have a garden, he will devour it. He eats and eats. Then he eats even more. Every person who knows how to tend a garden understands that caterpillars can devour plants in minutes. They eat and eat and eat. They fill up on food so much that their skin begins to stretch. Eventually, they shed their skin. Then, guess what happens next? Yep – the caterpillar goes back to eating. He eats more and more - and he just keeps living by this consuming desire. All he can think about is more. More. More. As this caterpillar's skin stretches out once again, he ends up shedding his skin *again*. Believe it or not, this process happens four times.

As human beings, we understand what it means to consume... or *over consume*. But God made us for more than just going through life ready to consume. Just as this caterpillar was made for more than consuming, you are too. God has dreams and designs for your life. He longs for you to live out your divine destiny. He wants you to get a hold of the vision for the life that he created for you to embody. And God knows that when you see the dream, the destiny, and the vision, it will capture your heart and reveal the pathway into your purpose. Your life is an unfolding story, and the choices you make today in your life will determine what stories you tell tomorrow.

The fifth time a caterpillar sheds his skin, he eats so much food that he finds himself crawling up a little tree. He is tired. He wants to take an afternoon nap. Don't we all? He's exhausted from all the eating... and growing. So he decides to enter the chrysalis. This is where something magnificent happens to the caterpillar. Upon entering the cocoon stage, this caterpillar has only fifty cells. Then, an amazing thing happens. A green goo overtakes him. He goes from fifty cells to 50,000 cells. He doesn't just change a little bit. He becomes something entirely new. He becomes something fundamentally different. Everything has changed.

For twelve to fourteen days, he stays in the cocoon until he has the strength to break out. When he breaks out, something unusual happens. He realizes something profound... he has wings. Just for fun, imagine if you indulged in large amounts of pizza and ice cream. After taking a nap for two weeks, imagine waking up with wings, and suddenly being able to use those wings to fly. At that point, I'm thinking life would be pretty spectacular. How about you?

At this stage, the once caterpillar has become a brand-new creature – a butterfly. This butterfly embraces its new form. For the first couple hours, the butterfly begins to stretch out his wings. He soon dries off. Once he comes out of the chrysalis and dries off his wings, do you want to know where these caterpillars go? The caterpillars want to go where I want to go right now – they go to Mexico. Wait, What!? They've never even known how to fly and suddenly they say, "I'm going to Mexico?" Must be nice. Sounds like a fun vacation to me! (this is unique to monarch butterflies)

Here's the thing: they have never flown before. The trek is 2,000 miles away. Somehow, they develop the strength in this process to take the journey: forty days, fifty miles per day. Most people see a butterfly and ponder its beauty as it glides through the sky with fluttering wings and amazing colors. They don't think much past that. They don't really know what's ahead for the butterfly.

One thing that's even more amazing is not just that these butterflies go to Mexico. Along the way, they stop to rest on flowers. What are they doing? They are pollinating. They are feeding. They are spreading seeds onto these flowers so that the flowers will continue to bloom. That's pretty cool.

This remarkable metaphor resembles how you and I can experience a new way of living and a new way of being. Humanity has an invitation from our Creator to live as a new creation. And that new way of living and being gets established through a personal relationship with our Creator. According to the Scriptures, we are made new *in Christ*.

> **The old has gone and the new has come.**
> *2 Corinthians 5:17*

The caterpillar to butterfly metaphor is a beautiful image from God's creation that illustrates what a human being can anticipate happening in their life when they choose to follow Jesus Christ. We begin to align ourselves with God's dreams and designs for our lives. Just like the caterpillar goes through a metamorphosis and leaves behind the old and becomes something entirely new (a butterfly), we can expect to do the same by the work of God in our lives. This transformation begins with a personal relationship with Jesus, and emerges as a life-changing reality where we flourish like never before.

When we step fully into life with God through a relationship with Jesus Christ, metamorphosis awaits us.

Whole life *transformation* becomes our new vision and new reality. The dreams and designs that God has for us spring forth. We find the pathway to our purpose and begin to discover our divine destiny. We find hope and peace like never before. We find courage and faith, joy and meaning. And ultimately, we find God's grace and love to be the all-consuming experience in our lives. And as we move deeper into knowing God personally, along with experiencing his grace and love, we also find what Jesus promises to his followers – *life to the fullest.*

To say it succinctly, Jesus offers humanity the greatest opportunity we could ever have. He invites us to follow him and then promises life transformation. When we decide to follow Christ, everything really does change. We leave our old way of life and enter the new way of living that is offered to us. We are reminded that God isn't satisfied with small improvements in our lives that are achieved only by human effort. God desires that we experience transformation from the inside out through the power of the Holy Spirit. The old way gets put behind us and the new way is fully embraced. That means new habits, new choices, new thinking, and new living.

So are you ready to find a new purpose, along with a new destiny? Because we would like to guide you into a journey to discover a completely new you. What will follow is a deeper, stronger, and better version of yourself! Along the way, you will develop different priorities and perspectives, as well as deeper passions and distinct pursuits. This new life awaits you if you choose this path.

> If you have really experienced the Anointed One, and heard his truth, *it will be seen in your life;* for we know that the ultimate reality is embodied in Jesus! And he has taught you to let go of the lifestyle of the ancient man, the old self-life, which was corrupted by sinful and deceitful desires that spring from delusions. Now it's time to be made new by every revelation that's been given to you. And to be transformed as you embrace the glorious Christ within as your new life and live in union with him! For God has recreated you all over again in his perfect righteousness, and you now belong to him in the realm of true holiness.
>
> *Ephesians 4:21-24*

When the monarch butterflies emerge, they become something entirely new. After they arrive in Mexico, there's a village on a 10,000-foot mountain range. It's where approximately 100,000,000 monarch butterflies descend. The butterflies have gone on this long journey, stopping along the way to pollinate and spread these seeds of goodness and beauty. And when they get to the village, guess what happens? Not only does the village welcome them all, there's a massive celebration! Sounds like heaven to me.

One day, there will be a celebration.

In the meantime, God has a plan and a purpose that involves your participation.

As you begin to experience God's transforming work in every aspect of your life, you will become a person who spreads the seeds of the Gospel to a world who doesn't yet know God. This is part of your divine destiny. God has a specific purpose for you that no one else can live out. When you step into this new life with God, you will be united with his tribe. And God will use you to spread the seeds of goodness, truth, and the beauty of God.

Your life is an untold story. A story that intersects the story of God.

Never forget that God created you as his masterpiece (Ephesians 2:10). You are an original (Galatians 5:26). You have been created by God for something so much more than you can imagine! So, over the next several weeks, if you welcome the Holy Spirit to do his work, get ready to encounter a deep and transformational work of God in your life!

What to Expect

Over the next six weeks, you will notice how purposeful we were in creating a daily format and weekly rhythm. While we want you to complete most of this on your own, it is also an experience that will be enhanced by going through it with others. We encourage you to carve out fifteen to twenty minutes per day to focus on personal growth. But we also recommend that you identify a small group to go on the growth journey with you. We suggest using your book individually, then coming together once per week to discuss what God is doing in your lives. Keep in mind, the more serious you take the daily practices and weekly community group experiences, the more significant impact it will have.

As you begin, identify a quiet place with minimal distractions. Make that the place you show up daily to engage your reading, prayer, and time alone with God. One thing that may help you settle your spirit each day is to take a few deep breaths as you begin. Inhale for a few seconds. Then, slowly exhale. Repeat that four or five times. In these moments of slowing your soul down and becoming silent, be mindful of God's presence. Go ahead and invite the Holy Spirit to speak to you as you read. Resist the impulse to hurry. Don't just try to get it over with. Slowing down your reading will help you absorb the meaning of the words and concepts. It will also create space to hear God's quiet, gentle whisper.

As you interact with the Scriptures each day, focus your heart and mind on the reality that you are reading what the Creator of the universe spoke into existence. The truths are dynamic and alive (Hebrews 4:12).. In 2 Timothy 3:16-17 we're told, "All scripture is inspired by God…" So, pay attention to how God speaks to you through the Bible, which are his very words. Listen for quiet inner promptings, stirrings in your soul, and to anything that moves your heart. Welcome the truth when it cuts to the core or convicts you of sin. Sometimes, God's Word fills you up and re-centers you. Other times, it will sting or surprise you. Through it all, God can bring transformation as you strive to respond to and apply what you're discovering. Along the way, don't forget to savor the work God is doing… and thank him for it all as it's happening.

The Weekly Schedule

We will provide seven daily practices as a guide to facilitate transformation in your life as you gain understanding and integrate what you're learning and experiencing. Know that we have prayed for you from the beginning of this book (and we will continue). God wants to interact with you as you read, reflect, gather, and pray – and he will when you invite him. Go ahead and anticipate a move of God in your life in the weeks ahead. Carry that expectancy with you.

If this learning experience seems heavy on structure, know that the structure is designed to serve you – and not to be rigid. We know that life doesn't always go the way we think it will. So use the structure in a way that's helpful. And feel free to adapt it as needed.

Day 1: Preparation

The first day of the weekly rhythm introduces you to the topic of the week, while also providing stories, concepts, and definitions to help you gain a clear understanding of the weekly theme. In addition, we will invite you to respond to some questions and jot down your thoughts and reflections. This will help you process what you're learning and identify how to apply it to your life. Let us also give you fair warning: we've intentionally written questions that we hope will challenge you. Some of them might make you uneasy. But from our vantage point, we can make these six weeks easy and comfortable, or we can pose some challenging questions that create space for God's Spirit to work deeply so that it can make a real difference in your life and the life of your community. Here's the good news – if you'll let it, these six weeks will cultivate a metamorphosis in your life – and perhaps in your surrounding community of friends.

Day 2: Study

On Day 2, we provide different passages from the Scriptures for you to read, meditate on, and study more deeply. We encourage you to read the verses *several times* and let the words come alive to you. If you allow the truth and meaning of the Scriptures to penetrate your soul through deeper meditation and study, you'll create space for God's Spirit to transform you along the way. Don't forget to slow down enough to engage with the commentary and respond to the questions. If there's a study of a Greek or Hebrew word, let that word and its meaning get embedded into your heart. Carry its meaning with you throughout the week – maybe it will come alive to you in a new way.

Day 3: Change
Day 3 will take you to the next level. We've introduced the concept of the week and seen the foundational truths around it in the Scriptures. Now, what does the core idea of the week really mean in *your life*? How would *your life* be different if you started to apply what you're learning? On Day 3, take time to participate in the journaling and reflection exercises that we suggest. The process of writing things down has been shown to help us remember things longer and allow things to truly take shape inside of us. Our hope is that Day 3 of each week will foster deeper introspection and thoughtfulness, which are pathways to genuine life change.

Day 4: Action
By Day 4, you'll likely have opened your *heart* to change, which is right where you want to be. But also consider how you're going to use your *hands and feet.* This day guides you in how to put what you're learning into practice. This is the most practical section, and it will require action steps. We'll provide some applications for you to consider, but God may stir up other applications that are unique to you and your life. It's critical that you follow through on these next steps. The success of your personal growth (and your group's growth) depends on your willingness to respond to and apply what you're learning. Scripture tells us that gaining knowledge alone will not produce transformation. Application is critical. Action is essential.

Day 5: Community
Day 5 is designed to be a model for how our lives – *in community* – are to be increasingly lived out. On this day, gather with others (people who are also putting these things into practice). If possible, share a meal together each week – it creates the

necessary space to cultivate stronger and better relationships. This whole process will be more difficult if you don't go through this experience with a few friends, so make the most of it. Healthy community, where people are committed to live on mission with God and each other, lies at the center of all we will be learning together.

Day 6: Focus

On Day 6, we will approach the theme of the week from a unique angle. We'll provide some additional thoughts for you to ponder as you continue to contemplate (and perhaps wrestle with) the theme of the week. Our intent is to help you pull some things together from that week and be reminded of the transformation that's possible in your life. This day will help to focus your heart, your mind, and your life on the priorities of God's kingdom.

Day 7: Rest

The last day in our weekly rhythm is meant for you to rest. This day is an important reminder, one that we as human beings tend to struggle with doing. We all need to take time to slow down on a regular basis to rest. This is a biblical pattern, and even a mandate from God – that we honor the Sabbath and keep it holy. Practicing the Sabbath is good for our soul. On this day, we're not asking you to respond to anything, obey anything, or take any action. We're simply inviting you to rest and recreate. That means you can simply invite God to fill you up as you sit with him and remain still.

We want to encourage you to rest in Jesus' completed work on your behalf. It's out of that rest that you will create value, beauty, and work.

The Sabbath reminds us that no one can earn God's approval. We create, work, and produce out of the soul rest that we experience in Christ. Just so you know – we intentionally keep Day 7 short and simple. That allows you to have time to be still and listen to the gentle whisper of God's Spirit that is often reminding you that you are loved. Most of us stay very busy. We often don't take adequate time listening to God. As a result, we sometimes fail to hear God's inner promptings. So, if you make the choice to refrain from hurrying on Day 7, we believe that you will cultivate a listening heart. And soon enough, you will also experience the presence and power of God in a unique and life-changing way.

A Community With a Cause

We've learned that it helps to give people time to process the tough, inner-life issues individually, and then come together communally. So, before you begin the process, pick a day that your community will meet. The goal is to increasingly live like a family on God's mission together throughout the week. What may start out as a weekly meeting can grow into a meaningful lifestyle that changes who you're becoming, how you relate to others, and what you do with your life. In other words, transformation awaits you through intentional community.

Want our suggestion? Choose a group of friends that you invite on a multi-week journey. Or, maybe you want to present this idea to a group that you're already part of (i.e. small group, life group, Bible study, house church, missional community, etc.). It's up to you on how you form this group, and if you go beyond the six weeks. But a six-week commitment is a good place to start.

While there aren't any limitations on the number of people you can have in your group, we've found that between six and twelve people is a range that works well for small group dynamics.

A group this size can typically fit in most homes, apartments, or around a table. It is conducive for all to participate in discussions. It is big enough to accommodate an occasional absentee and it is small enough to share simple meals without massive hours spent planning. The group can include people who are in all different stages spiritually. It can range from brand new Jesus followers to mature Jesus followers. It can also include those who are still sorting things out when it comes to faith but have a curiosity to learn and grow. All ages and all backgrounds can participate on this discipleship endeavor.

The clear and compelling mission that Jesus sends his followers on is a disciple-making mission. As he invites humanity to be his disciples, he simultaneously challenges us to make disciples. He envisions this all happening in the context of community. These mission-minded communities are ultimately postured to serve and love the world, as the Holy Spirit transforms our lives along the way.

WEEK 1

AN UNUSUAL CHOICE

You did not choose me, but I chose you...
John 15:16

PREPARATION

As I (Steve) began college at the University of South Carolina, I was determined to clarify what my career pursuit was going to be. Once I resolved that matter and decided on my degree, I still found myself longing for something more. But that unsettling feeling that I was experiencing inside became the impetus that caused me to enter a season of self-reflection. I soon realized how deep my longing to find purpose really went. I wanted so badly for my life to count. I wanted to live a life that made a difference, that left a mark on this world. And along with that, I knew that I needed to become someone different than I was.

As a young adult, I was at a crossroads. Maybe you've been there too. For me, I knew something had to change. I knew I had to change. More than that, I sensed that God might have something to say about where my life was headed. And I knew that I couldn't change on my own. I needed God. These longings and reflections led me on a new quest that would eventually change everything about my life. It would alter the entire trajectory of my journey.

One night, I was just hanging out with a few friends in my dorm room – but I recognized that this evening was atypical. I had been paying closer attention to my newly awakened desires, and on that night, things culminated. When my friends went out, I was strangely compelled to stay home. I told them I wasn't feeling great and was going to stay back. After giving me a hard time, they eventually left without me. Then, I walked to the side of my bed and fell to my knees in prayer. Best I could tell, God had been drawing me towards him in the weeks leading up to that moment, and it was on that night that things converged like never before. It's hard to fully explain that night, but I had an undeniable encounter with God in my dorm room in Columbia, South Carolina. It was as if God became real to me in a whole new way. I felt his presence. I somehow knew God was with me and working within me. Somewhere deep inside, I knew that I needed to start to seek God if I was going to find my purpose and become who I was created to be. That night everything changed for me – I made a focused commitment of my life to Jesus Christ, no turning back!

A few days later, I met Kevin. He was a quarterback on the Gamecock football team. I shared my story with him and told him that I had just become a Christian. Naturally, he was excited and celebrated my decision. Then, what Kevin said to me has completely shaped my life and my understanding about following Jesus. Kevin told me:

"Don't become a Christian. Become a disciple."

At first, I didn't know exactly what he meant. But after he elaborated, I got it. In essence, this is what Kevin was saying:

> We don't need any more Christians. What we need are disciples. When Jesus says, "Come, follow me," he's inviting us to embrace the Gospel, and with a grateful response, make a focused commitment of our entire life to follow him, his teachings, and his mission. Jesus wasn't simply interested in asking people to "believe the right things" or "behave like a good moral *Christian*." His desire encompassed so much more. He designed every human being with remarkable intention, to live out their divine purpose, and to experience life to the fullest – a way of life that can only be found in and through Christ. God longs to transform us from the inside out. He wants us to become women and men of

Christ-like character, so we become reflections of him for his glory. Jesus invites all humanity into a new way of living, one that changes everything about our lives – our eternal destiny, our relationships, our character, our identity, and our purpose. As we encounter life transformation, God wants to use us as conduits of his love to help others discover how the Gospel can bring the same kind of hope and life transformation. In essence, he wants to bless us so we can bless others. He wants to change us so we can help others change – but it starts on the inside. It starts with our response to the Gospel. And when that happens, we learn how to live a life that flows from the Gospel. It's Gospel-living, and it'll change everything about your life.

Then Kevin said:

"Unfortunately, that's not what describes the life of most Christians. But it does describe the life of a disciple… at least as we were intended to live. As I have learned and embraced this reality, that's how I have discovered my calling and my purpose. And Steve, that's where the calling on your life begins. If you miss this truth, you miss everything."

What Kevin told me that night profoundly impacted me. Even today, I'm grateful that God sent him into my life to show me what it means to be a disciple of Christ. He cast the vision – and I got it like never before. He also didn't leave me there. Kevin took time in the weeks and months ahead to build a friendship with me. He cared enough to spend time investing in me as a person. He showed me love and guided me into wisdom. He carved out space in his life to pass on what he had learned. He shared what he was experiencing with God with someone who wasn't as far along in their journey. Not only did he live as a disciple, he lived as a disciple maker who modeled the life that Jesus invites all of his followers to embody – to be disciples who make other disciples.

It's unfortunate that there are far too many professed Christians who settle for "being a good, moral, Christian person" and who reduce Christianity to believing certain things yet never becoming true disciples. Being a Christian is far more than what the western world has made it to be. In the western world, you can refer to yourself as a Christian yet show no signs of progress towards becoming a disciple. That means that discipleship really isn't a condition for becoming a Christian.

Somewhere along the way, we have mistakenly made it acceptable in the church to be a Christian but not a disciple.

To me, this is a spiritual tragedy. It's almost as if we view being a disciple as something that some Christians do when they are more committed to the church or to ministry. But according to the teachings of Jesus (and the whole Bible), this is not the case. When Jesus says, "follow me," he is inviting us to surrender our will and agenda, and to get on board with who he is and what he's about. Our lives aren't intended to be done our way and according to our will. We were created to discover and do his will and to live his way. And to the measure that we do, we will experience more joy, more peace, more love, and more hope. We will experience true transformation and discover our divine destiny.

This may be a surprise to you, but the Bible never defines the word *Christian*, nor does anyone ever get asked to become a *Christian*. Not by Jesus, not by the original disciples, and not even by the Apostle Paul who scribed about half the New Testament. The term *Christian* only gets used three times in the entire New Testament. In all three cases, the word is used with negative connotations in reference to early Jesus followers who were being persecuted harshly and seen as a disruption to society. Interestingly, even the term *Christian* was never used by followers of Jesus to describe themselves. Instead, the word was used solely by people outside the Jesus community to describe people inside the Jesus community. Isn't that interesting?

In contrast, there is a word that gets used in the New Testament to appropriately describe followers of Jesus. What is that word? You guessed it... *disciple*. This word gets used 269 times in the New Testament.

To say it simply, the New Testament doesn't teach people how to become Christians, rather, it calls us to be disciples... and *disciples-makers*. And just so we're clear and on the same page, the call to become a disciple was not only a central focus in Jesus' life and teachings – that theme and emphasis is also threaded throughout the entire New Testament.

To better understand what it means to be a disciple, we're going to go back in time and enter the first century in hopes of gaining deeper insights from the origins of discipleship. We're going to look at the impact discipleship had on people and the surrounding culture. Then, we'll look more closely at how it all affects our lives today, including what the applications are for you and me.

Self-Reflection

1. If we asked one hundred Christians to define what it means to be a Christian, how many of them would have different answers? How about you? What would *you* say if someone asked you, "*What is a Christian?*"
In two or three sentences, go ahead and jot down your answers.

2. Now, take a couple minutes to think about who, or what, shaped your definition of a Christian and your view of Christianity *the most* – i.e. life experiences, people, churches, church leaders or traditions, or any part of your background. Also consider the influence of your family, friends, church and/or denominational background, the culture or subculture you were raised in, and mentors and/or pastors that influenced you. Jot down a few of your reflections.

3. If you consider yourself a Christian, what has changed about your life since your decision to follow Jesus? Perhaps you can reflect on your daily behaviors, your approach to work or finances, or how you talk to or about others. Or, maybe think about how your daily and weekly habits, or passions and priorities have changed, or even how you handle conflict. There are many aspects to how God changes us. For

1.1 Preparation

now, just write about some of the changes that have taken place in your life since becoming a Christian. Be reminded that we can always tell our true beliefs by the actions, habits, and behaviors of our lives, not simply by what we profess to believe.

4. Now, take a stab at explaining the distinct differences between what *most people* believe it means to be a Christian versus what it means to be a disciple. If you are newer to understanding what it means to be a disciple, no problem. For now, we're just establishing a baseline. In the weeks to come, chances are that all of us will have our definitions recalibrated and realigned to one degree or another. Because, when we dig into the teachings of Jesus, we will always be challenged to change. Go ahead and write down how you would differentiate what it means to be a *Christian* versus what it means to be a *disciple*.

5. What is your response to this quote? In what ways do you think it's true? "The cost of discipleship is indeed great. But the cost of non discipleship is far greater" (Dallas Willard).

1.2 STUDY

In the first century, the idea of discipleship didn't exist in Judea, nor was it practiced in Babylon or Egypt (at least not early on). Discipleship did permeate Galilee, more specifically, a small but significant rural town called Capernaum. About 2,000 people lived there. And although it wasn't his place of birth, it was Jesus' hometown. It was also where discipleship remained central and of supreme importance. In fact, most first-century people considered Capernaum the hub of discipleship.

Isn't it interesting that Jesus left the small mountainous village of Nazareth and chose to make this modest village in Galilee the place for his public ministry (See Matthew 4:12–17)? And it's fascinating to know that the people in Capernaum weren't known for being sophisticated, educated, or cultured. Rather, they were known for their remarkable *passion*.

Capernaum might have been small in size but it was big in passion. The synagogue and the Scriptures were of massive importance. What mattered most to the people in this village was zealous discussion and engaging debate on spiritual and theological matters - for instance, the meaning of Scripture, how to live by faith, and the implications of the coming Messiah.

According to Jewish history and tradition, many great rabbis practiced their teaching and selected their disciples in and around Capernaum. Rabbis went there to find disciples. Potential disciples went there to find rabbis. Ultimately, it was where the best and the brightest rabbis would go to find the best and brightest disciples.

Isn't it interesting that this is where Jesus chose to go – where the highest level of learning was happening? Seems like he must have wanted to walk among the best of the best. And so, we find Jesus stepping into this context. Considering that everything Jesus did was with great intention, doesn't this make you want to know why God chose to use the Galilean discipleship model?

During the first century, to become a rabbi was the highest honor in Jewish culture. Virtually every young Jewish boy aspired to become a rabbi. As one might expect, the only way to become a rabbi was to become a disciple of an already existing rabbi.

Many scholars note that when a boy was just ten years old, it was likely that he had already memorized the first five books of our modern-day Old Testament: Genesis, Exodus, Leviticus, Numbers, and Deuteronomy. I don't mean he memorized the names of those books. Those boys knew every word of the Torah (Genesis through Deuteronomy). Essentially, boys started learning the Hebrew Scriptures before they could walk.

Somewhere between age ten and fourteen, **many of these young adolescents sought to memorize the rest of the Hebrew Scriptures**... that is, our modern-day Old Testament. Rather impressive!

By about the age of fourteen, **a Jewish boy was ready to approach a rabbi** if he demonstrated his exceptional knowledge of the Scriptures and showed himself to be a standout among his peers. With their goal of becoming a rabbi clear, the boy's only path to achieve that goal was to be selected as a disciple of a rabbi.

As you can see, this method of discipleship was demanding. And it only rewarded the best and brightest. To be selected, you had to prove yourself to a rabbi. You had to show enough acumen and proficiency. Ultimately, you had to perform well enough for the rabbi to be willing to pull you into his orbit and invest his life in you.

Somewhere about the age of fifteen, a Jewish boy would be ready to approach a rabbi whom he thought he could be like. There were typically plenty of rabbis who these teenagers and young adults thought that they could not be like – or who they didn't want to be like. But when they identified the rabbi that they aspired to emulate, the boy knew he needed to patiently listen to this rabbi for a season. He anxiously waited, hoping to be noticed by him. He held on to hope that he would be approved as someone who had what it took to become a disciple of that rabbi.

Rabbis were not all that easy to please, as they were quite particular. Not only did they want disciples who they believed could emulate their way of living, they were looking for disciples who could be trained to *take on their yoke.* Their yoke was their perspective or interpretation of the Scriptures. In essence, they desired to "make disciples" who would spread their message to as many people as possible. But again, these rabbis would only choose those whom they *really believed* could take on their yoke in proficient and competent ways. They would only select disciples in whom they had confidence. They needed to know that a disciple could live up to their expectations and make a good name for them.

There were different methods that helped the rabbi decide whether or not he would select an ambitious Jewish boy. One method came through interactive question-asking. This was a skill that young Jewish boys began to learn early on. For instance, the rabbi might ask a question about a text from the Hebrew Scriptures (what we know today as a verse). He wanted the potential disciple to respond by asking another question that revealed that he knew right where that verse was. For instance, the rabbi may ask a question using a line from Leviticus. Then, he'd expect the potential disciple to respond with another question that showed his knowledge of the verses in Leviticus that came before and after the line.

Though this may seem odd to us, it was a familiar way of interacting in that culture. And, it was a good way to test the potential disciple's knowledge and sharpness of mind. Ultimately, it was a test of *performance* that rabbis used with the Jewish teenagers and young adults who would do their best to stand in that space and meet the rabbi's expectations, hoping to be approved of and chosen by the one they admired and aspired to be like. It was intense – a high-pressure situation.

After the boy followed this rabbi around and listened to the chosen rabbi's teachings (which typically lasted about six months), **he would eventually ask the rabbi, "May I follow you?"** He was asking whether the rabbi believed that he had what it takes to be just like him and to carry on his message. I can just imagine how much the anxiety levels rose in these young men. After all, their dream was hanging in the balance. There was a lot on the line. This was a big moment in their life.

In most cases, the rabbi would say something like, "**God has gifted you. And you're a godly young man who knows the Scriptures. However, it's time for you to go home and apply your trade.**" In other words, I don't think you have the skills, knowledge, or abilities that you need to be like me or to take on my yoke. The rabbi would then encourage him to continue in his study of the Scriptures every day. He would exhort him to strive to become the godliest fisherman (or potter, carpenter, etc.) in all of Galilee.

In that moment, the boy's lifelong dream was shattered. Imagine how many of those young men walked away feeling like a failure. Huge discouragement would set in, perhaps even despair. I imagine that some would spiral into depression because they had worked their whole life for that moment – and it was as if it disappeared before their eyes. All hope and anticipation of a bright future vanished. In essence, the message they heard was that they didn't have what it takes. And that message can crush you. They walked away feeling that they didn't perform well enough to be chosen.

In contrast, there were the rare few who did perform well enough. They were approved of. They were chosen by the rabbi, and felt affirmed. These potential disciples had pursued the rabbi and waited around for his full acceptance. With their life dream hanging in the balance, when that rabbi thought they had what it takes, he would choose that boy. Everything would change for him and his family at that moment.

To the ones the rabbi deemed competent, to the ones he considered worthy of accepting, to the ones who performed better than all the rest, the rabbi would say, "Come follow me."

Sound familiar?

The boy's dream had come true for him *and his family*. Then, as a response, the boy would prepare to leave his family, his village, and the local synagogue where he had been studying. Essentially, he would leave everything to follow that rabbi. After all, he had been focused on this dream for his whole life. And now, he was fully ready to give up whatever was needed to follow his rabbi. He now sought to *take on his yoke* and become *just like him.*

In many cases, the new *disciple* would start to live with his new rabbi for a season because he was so devoted to following him

around as much as possible. His life obsession was learning how to emulate his rabbi in every way. And now, he carried the burden of spreading the message of his rabbi to all who would listen.

1.3 CHANGE

Although Jesus embedded himself into the first-century discipleship tradition of Capernaum, there were some discipleship components that he deconstructed and redefined. In particular, he didn't wait for others to approach him, nor did he try to evaluate the level of performance of the prospective disciples. He didn't base anything on their competence, knowledge, or good morality. Jesus didn't want these young and aspiring rabbis to doubt whether he would approve of them based on what they could do or not do. His approach was counter-cultural. His philosophy flipped the Galilean model on its head.

Instead of having to prove themselves worthy, smart enough, or of highest competence, Jesus took a new initiative. He sought out others. He decided to be the one who did the choosing without having others prove themselves. And even further, the ones he sought and selected weren't the people others thought he would select. His choices were *unusual*.

Many of the early disciples whom Jesus selected were simple Galilean fishermen. They were unlearned, and at times even ignorant. Most were rough around the edges. Some were even elementary. Plus, these guys were often governed by their Jewish passions and prejudices. The early disciples often remained narrow in their perspective and foolish in their thinking. Sure, many of these knuckleheads were the age of high schoolers (and others were young adults), so we'll let them off the hook a little bit. But when Jesus comes along, he could have chosen anyone he wanted. Yet, what does he do? He chooses the misfits who were described in the book of Acts as "ordinary, unschooled men." In fact, they had most likely already been passed up by other rabbis. Yet, Jesus didn't look past them for a second - because he wasn't looking for the valedictorians. He wasn't searching for superstar performers. His goal wasn't to get the smartest and most talented people in the room to carry out his message. Quite the contrary. Jesus looked past the external and selected those who he knew could be transformed on the inside.

Jesus' selection process was never based on performance or morality. No one had to earn anything from him. What Jesus did turned the Galilean discipleship philosophy and approach upside down.

The Origins of Transformation

According to the chronology of Luke's Gospel, we know that Jesus' reputation preceded him. That means, when he invited the first disciples to follow him, he had already raised a dead person and cast out demons. So it isn't the first time Jesus met these guys. The four gospels tell us that he had already interacted with some of them in Judea. Some had even followed Jesus (as well as John the Baptist) around town already. So they knew who Jesus was when this divine intersection emerged. And those Jesus encounters changed their lives forever.

Here's how the transformation of these first disciples started:

> And passing along by the Sea of Galilee, he saw Simon and Andrew the brother of Simon casting a net in the sea; for they were fishermen. And Jesus said to them, **"Follow me and I will make you become fishers of men."** And immediately they left

> their nets and followed him. And going on a little farther, he saw James the son of Zebedee and John his brother, who were in their boat mending the nets. And immediately he called them; and they left their father Zebedee in the boat with the hired servants, and followed him.
>
> *Mark 1:16-20 RSV*

When Jesus said, "come follow me" to Peter and Andrew, they immediately dropped their nets and followed.

Then he called James and John – who *immediately* left their boat and their father to follow Jesus.

Peter and Andrew were casting their nets into the sea, throwing circular nets out over each side of the boat trying to catch fish. This suggests that they will become people who cast out the Gospel to the world around them. We find out later that Andrew becomes the disciple who leads people to Jesus, even bringing his own brother to Christ. Down the road, we also discover that Peter becomes the great evangelist who preached the Gospel to 3,000 people on the day of Pentecost.

When Jesus called James and John, they were mending their nets. "Mending" is the same Greek word that appears in Ephesians 4, where Paul writes that pastors/teachers are to "equip" (or mend) the saints to do the work of the ministry (Eph. 4:12). Mending and equipping are the kinds of work we eventually see James and John doing throughout the New Testament.

When Jesus calls us, he promises to mend us and equip us. In addition, he takes full responsibility to teach and train us in everything we need to know and do in order to fulfill his purposes in and through our lives. We begin by becoming disciples and are soon trained how to make disciples. Jesus is telling us that we were made for this!

1.4 ACTION

Have you ever wondered: what exactly did Jesus see in those first disciples?

Well, it seems that he must have seen people who were not only unique but who were willing to be changed. They were hungry for something more in their life. And it seems that he must have believed that they would be willing to give themselves to something bigger than their own life – to God's bigger purposes. Apparently, Jesus believed in who they could become and what he could do in and through them if they would surrender their lives to him. He saw past what others looked at and envisioned what others could not. Apparently he saw their potential and deemed it worth his time and energy to invest his life in them. He knew that they were *made for more!*

When Jesus selected these first disciples, he assumed full responsibility to teach and train them in an entirely new way of living – what we might call *kingdom living.* Jesus spent more than three years making disciples of these young, not yet men. He called them not only to be his disciples but to turn around and begin making other disciples… as imperfect and ordinary as they were.

In essence, Jesus pulled together this ragtag group of young, soon-to-be adults to do something great in the world. He must have thought to himself, "with the help and power of God's Spirit, these guys can become just like me! Because they have hearts that are open and willing, I can use them to change the course of human history."

Jesus Christ believed in their potential to change despite all of their imperfections, limitations, and weaknesses.

And guess what? Jesus believes the same thing about you. It's why he also chose you to be his disciple.

> "You did not choose me. I chose you…"
>
> John 15:16

Imagine Jesus approaching these guys on the beach. As he stands in front of these ordinary, unschooled young men, they must have felt his deep and tender love for them. Just think about that moment when Jesus unexpectedly invites them to follow him into a new way of living and being. They knew they hadn't earned it, nor felt they deserved it. Yet, Jesus is still fond of them. And of all of the people he could have chosen, these are the ones he selected. When my son was a toddler, I would often tell him when I was tucking them in, "If I lined up all the little boys and girls in the whole wide world, and I could pick just one, who do you think I would select?" After just a few times doing that, he would say, "ME!" with an enormous smile on his cute little face. In a childlike way, he was reminded in that moment how much his father loved him.

Just when these first disciples thought they had been passed up, and perhaps felt rejected by that, Jesus makes **an unusual choice**. Likely, they felt how much Jesus loved them. And it's probably that they are overwhelmed at that moment. Yet, it's clear that they are ready to follow him, no turning back. As they step into this destiny changing moment, they eagerly anticipate what's over the horizon. They know their lives are about to change. They might even sense that the world is about to change.

An Undivided Passion

It's fascinating that these first disciples left their nets and their families. To be clear, this invitation wasn't about getting them to leave their fishing careers behind nor to force them to abandon their families. In fact, we know from the gospels that these guys later went back to being fishermen. We also know that James and John didn't abandon their family. Jesus is making a point that when he calls us to follow him, he's calling us to make him, his teachings, and his mission our highest priority. Our career, our family, and anything else in our lives, become secondary when compared to Jesus being our ultimate passion. Jesus followers are undivided in their devotion to their Rabbi.

Although they made mistakes along the way (we will too), they stayed the course (except for Judas). Yes, we are imperfect, sin-marred people. But that doesn't disqualify us. In fact, it's just who God wants to call and then use to advance the kingdom of God in human history. God is looking for people who acknowledge their sin, yet receive the forgiveness and mercy of God as they welcome him to transform who they are and what their lives are all about. His offer to you and to me is a new destiny, a new purpose, and a new way of living. When we follow Jesus with undivided passion, we'll inevitably begin to reflect him in how we live. We'll be motivated to serve and glorify him in ever-increasing ways. We'll begin to learn from him how to live just like him. That's what disciples do. That's who disciples are.

Self-Reflection

When we compare Jesus' approach to the cultural approach of first-century rabbis, it reminds us how the Gospel compares to other religions in our day. Other religions tell people what they have to do to earn approval or acceptance from God; or what they must do to make it to the afterlife. But the Gospel turns religion upside down. It reveals what Jesus has already accomplished for us – i.e. Jesus died on the cross for our sins and rose from the dead so that we could have *LIFE* - eternal and abundant *LIFE!* The Gospel declares that we are *already* accepted and loved, not because of anything we've done, but because of what he has done for us.

> He came to save us. Not because of any virtuous deed that we have done but only because of his extravagant mercy.
>
> *Titus 3:5*

> For by grace you have been saved by faith. Nothing you did could ever earn this salvation, for it was the love gift from God that brought us to Christ! So no one will ever be able to boast, for salvation is never a reward for good works or human striving.
>
> *Ephesians 2:8-9*

You are deemed worthy by God, not because of what you have done, but because of what God has done for you.

Genesis tells us that we are created in his image, with infinite and unchanging worthiness. And despite our sin, imperfections and brokenness, the Gospel brings grace and mercy to all who will open their hearts to receive it. This is a gift from God that cannot be earned, only received. Let that really sink in – salvation is a gift of grace to people who have missed the mark over and over again, to people who are marred by sin, to people who are broken, imperfect, and perhaps who even feel *ordinary* or *unusual.* The Gospel is hope and love to people who know they don't deserve God's love and acceptance. But, it isn't based on what we are able to do or not do. It's based on what God has already done on the Cross. So, we ought not boast of what we've done, but instead, respond with gratitude for his grace and mercy as we gain a fuller understanding of the ultimate sacrifice that Jesus Christ made for us.

Another translation of Ephesians 2:8-9 says it like this:

> God saved you by his grace when you believed. And you can't take credit for this; it is a gift from God. Salvation is not a reward for the good things we have done, so none of us can boast about it.

On a scale of one to ten:

1. How grateful are you that our loving Heavenly Father chose you? Explain.

2. How hungry are you in regards to your desire to learn from Jesus Christ about how to live in a new and entirely different way? In other words, write down where you are today in regards to the strength of your passion and desire for Christ. It's okay to be honest. .

3. How eagerly are you anticipating the transforming work of God in your life? What are you longing for God to change in your life? Explain.

4. How passionately are you pursuing a relationship with Jesus Christ today? What does that look like in your life right now? Explain.

Take a few moments to write out a prayer of gratitude in the space provided. After writing out your prayer, go ahead and pray it out loud to your Heavenly Father.

1.5 COMMUNITY

As your group gathers, we recommend sharing a meal together. After that, take a few minutes to share any "lightbulb moments" or "highlights" that arose as you engaged with this week's content. Then, read the following text (out loud as a group) before opening the floor for discussion.

The following text from Luke's Gospel is intended to foster reflection and discussion. Pay close attention to what it says in regards to being a disciple.

> As Jesus and his disciples were on their way, he came to a village where a woman named Martha opened her home to him. She had a sister called Mary, who sat at the Lord's feet listening to what he said. But Martha was distracted by all the preparations that had to be made. She came to him and asked, "Lord, don't you care that my sister has left me to do the work by myself? Tell her to help me!"
>
> "Martha, Martha," the Lord answered, "you are worried and upset about many things, but few things are needed – or indeed only one. Mary has chosen what is better, and it will not be taken away from her."
>
> *Luke 10:38-42*

Discuss: What are your *initial observations* after reading this passage?

The Cultural Context

For a few moments, let's dig a little deeper into the cultural context. One phrase that was commonly used in first-century culture was the concept of "sitting at someone's feet." This idea involved the establishment of a close relationship between a disciple and a rabbi. The phrase wasn't intended to describe Mary's physical location in the room, rather to tell you that Mary had made *a fundamental decision about her life.* She has made a focused commitment to Jesus Christ, which impacts the entire way she engages life, starting with developing a heart posture of humility and a perspective of gratitude. To sit at the feet of Jesus meant that Mary embodied a passion to learn from and receive from Jesus. She sat at the Lord's feet because she was seeking to become *just like Jesus* in every way possible. That doesn't mean she wanted to be religious. It meant that she had established a personal relationship with Jesus Christ. Part of her journey involved observing him in everyday moments, in hopes that she would discover how to live more like him in the context of that relationship. This is how disciples live.

It's important to recognize that we can be ***sitting at Jesus' feet*** when we're kneeling in prayer, but also when we're making our child's lunch, sending a text message, eating a meal with a friend, posting something on social media, exercising, or even watching Netflix.

In every nook and cranny of life, we can invite Jesus to be with us in the present moment – to be our Teacher, our Master, our Guide.

We're reminded that following Jesus isn't about becoming part of a specific religion, nor simply ascribing to a set of beliefs. Jesus is looking for a heart that receives him as a gift and then seeks him with gratitude and humility, striving to learn how to live like he lives in every way possible. Most of all, Jesus wants to be in a personal relationship with you… every day of your life. He longs for you to include and involve him in every aspect of your normal, day-to-day life.

Discuss: At times, do you find it difficult to see God present and at work in the ordinary aspects and activities of your life? Why is it challenging to integrate him into certain aspects of your life? What can help you take on that approach as you move forward in your relationship with God?

Sitting at His Feet

In our day, the mechanics of *sitting at Jesus'* feet looks different than it did in the first century. However, the priorities remain the same – Jesus is the focus. When we sit at his feet, we decide to make him our Lord and Leader. We surrender our right to maintain control as we submit our will to his will. Life becomes about doing it God's way, not our own way. To sit at the feet of Jesus means that he is always our first priority, and everything else flows from that. We are *undivided*. That doesn't mean we won't ever lose focus, but ultimately, we have become fully devoted followers of Jesus Christ. When we fail to honor God in some aspect of our lives, we live in the reality of his grace, invite him into our mess, and watch how he works to transform and restore us as we confess our sins to him and receive his mercy. That also means we can engage with God without condemnation and shame, for "there is no condemnation for those who are in Christ" (Romans 8:1).

Throughout the four gospels, Jesus calls his followers to seek first him and his kingdom above all else (Matthew 6:33). Living as a Christ-follower isn't a part-time obligation for a disciple, nor was it ever intended to be a casual commitment. Being a disciple cannot and should not be reduced to attending church on Sunday, or even to volunteering weekly or being involved in a small group Bible study (though all those things are good practices for Jesus followers). Following Jesus has always been intended to be an all-consuming reality that pervades every aspect of a disciple's life. When one chooses to follow Jesus, he becomes our primary focus and supreme authority. Along the way, God transforms our **passions, perspectives, pursuits**, and **priorities**. Ultimately, Jesus guides us into discovering *our* purpose, and how it aligns with *his* purpose.

Discuss:

- Describe one person you know who is a passionate, devoted Jesus follower. What do you admire about his or her life?

- On a scale of one to ten, what's your current level of passion in following Jesus? It's good to be honest and transparent.

- As a Jesus-follower, what passions, perspectives, pursuits, or priorities have changed since you started following him?

- From today's study and discussion, what do you sense that God wants to change in your life? What does he seem to be stirring up inside your heart?

Followers of Jesus are **God-guided, God-taught**, and **God-inspired**. So, as you move forward in your faith, remember that the Holy Spirit will teach and train you along the way, not only in how to be a disciple, but also in how to make disciples.

Go ahead and take a few minutes to pray for one another to close out your time together.

1.6 FOCUS

The Gospel of Mark tells us that Jesus chose the Twelve "in order that they may be with him" (3:14). He knew that the only way these ordinary, unschooled men could become just like him is if they began to live in close proximity to him. It was all about relational proximity, which is what ensued for three years. These twelve disciples spent those years watching, listening, and learning from Jesus in everyday life. They observed how to live like he lives and do what he does. But of course, they didn't always get it right. They messed up… a lot. Yet, this didn't surprise or discourage Jesus. From the outset, he knew that his disciples were flawed, imperfect, and at times, ignorant, foolish, and hard-headed. Jesus' love for them never changed. And he never stopped believing in them!

Today, Jesus is still looking for disciples – women and men – who don't have it all together. In actuality, Jesus looks for people who are aware of their brokenness and flawed nature. He looks for people who humbly acknowledge their powerlessness and know they need a strength that's beyond themselves. Jesus is looking for people who are hungry to learn, grow, and change. He's beckoning people who acknowledge their need for grace and who want to cultivate a personal relationship with their Creator.

Jesus invites us to embrace the gift that the Gospel is, and in grateful response and by his grace alone, seek him with every ounce of our being.

Jesus isn't highly selective in choosing his disciples. Instead, he is radically inclusive, as he invites all humanity into a relationship with him. And for those of us who receive and act on the invitation to follow him, God will empower us by the Holy Spirit, directing and instructing us with his Word and infusing their hearts with an undivided passion to live on mission with him.

Truth is, Jesus risked his reputation in the first century on people who were flawed and imperfect. But to him, it was worth it – 1,000 times over. And just as Jesus took a risk on his original disciples, he also takes a risk on you. Always remember that nothing about you surprises Jesus, nor does it deter his belief in you or love for you. He chose you not because you made yourself worthy, and not because you were competent or even good enough. Instead, he chose you because he simply loves you - unconditionally. He chose you because he believes in you profoundly. He has confidence that with God's transforming grace and power, you can become just like him. And guess what? He's also excited to partner with you in his mission. That means you have a unique calling and distinct purpose for your life. Your path to discover God's purpose and calling begins when you devote yourself fully to God, no turning back.

The most significant pursuit that the church can make in our day is for the people who consider themselves Christians to truly become authentic disciples of Jesus Christ - in the way that Jesus taught it, lived it, and envisioned it.

So remember: don't just become a Christian – become a disciple!

1.7 REST

On one occasion, Jesus invites his disciples to experience rest for their souls. It's a deep, inward rest, a kind of rest that we all need. He tells us how to find that rest, a type of rest that every disciple needs to experience if they want to live life to the fullest.

> **Come to me, all you who are weary and burdened, and I will give you rest.** Take my yoke upon you and learn from me, for I am gentle and humble in heart, and **you will find rest for your souls. For my yoke is easy and my burden is light.**
>
> *Matthew 11:28-30*

In the ancient near east, a yoke was something that was put on the ox so it could carry the plow or the wagon. This became the heavy burden of the ox. In parallel fashion, Jesus uses the metaphor of the yoke as a reminder that we all yoke ourselves to things that eventually become burdensome. They could be bad things. Or they could be good things that we wrongly make our *ultimate thing*.

If you want to know what you are yoked to, ask yourself: what (or who) are you living for? Is there anything that has mastered you or imprisoned you? Is there anything that you find your worth and value in? That's what you're yoked to.

And by the way, no one is unyoked. Whatever we attach ourselves to in order to derive our value and worth is what we're yoked to. And it's never enough. If we're yoked to our career, we might make the quality of our work the worth of our life. We carry this burden with us every day, often preoccupied by it. Then, if things don't go well with our work, we may feel empty or feel depressed. We might experience increasing anxiety and feelings of unworthiness. Or, you could be yoked to a person. It could be a relationship in your life that you keep clinging to in hopes that you will feel worthy or special. And perhaps you even compromise your values so that you fill that void.

In sum, whatever you are living for reveals what or who you are yoked to.

When Jesus comes along and says, "take **MY** yoke upon you…." followed by, "my yoke is easy and my burden is light," he's offering something to us that we all desperately need. He's offering a solution that only he can offer.

> Isn't it interesting that he doesn't tell us to pray more… nor muster up more faith. And he doesn't require us to try harder to do it on our own.

Instead, Jesus invites us to "sit at his feet," which is the only place that we'll find rest for our souls.

> It cannot be found anywhere else.

> He says, "Let go of self-sufficiency… and stop trying to do it on your own. If you will fix your eyes on me, soul-rest and deep fulfillment will come your way."

> In essence, he's telling us, "Remain relationally connected to me and I will show up in that space with you to provide rest."

One translation says it like this:

> Are you tired? Worn out? Burned out on religion? Come to me. Get away with me and you'll recover your life. I'll show you how to take a real rest. Walk with me and work with me – watch how I do it. Learn the unforced rhythms of grace. I won't lay anything heavy or ill-fitting on you. Keep company with me and you'll learn to live freely and lightly.
> *Matthew 11:28-30 MSG*

A Prayer of Blessing Over You

May you always remember that in your pursuit of God, he longs for you to find rest in him, remembering that he has chosen you not because of what you can do for him, but because he loves you. He really does love you just because you are you – and that reality can change everything about your life. May you know and experience the deep and profound truth of God's love. And by his grace, may the Gospel transform who you are and how you live. May the rushing river of God's amazing love flow in and through you this week... and for many weeks to come. It is in the ongoing experience of God's love that you will find the deepest strength.

WEEK 2
AN UNWAVERING CONNECTION

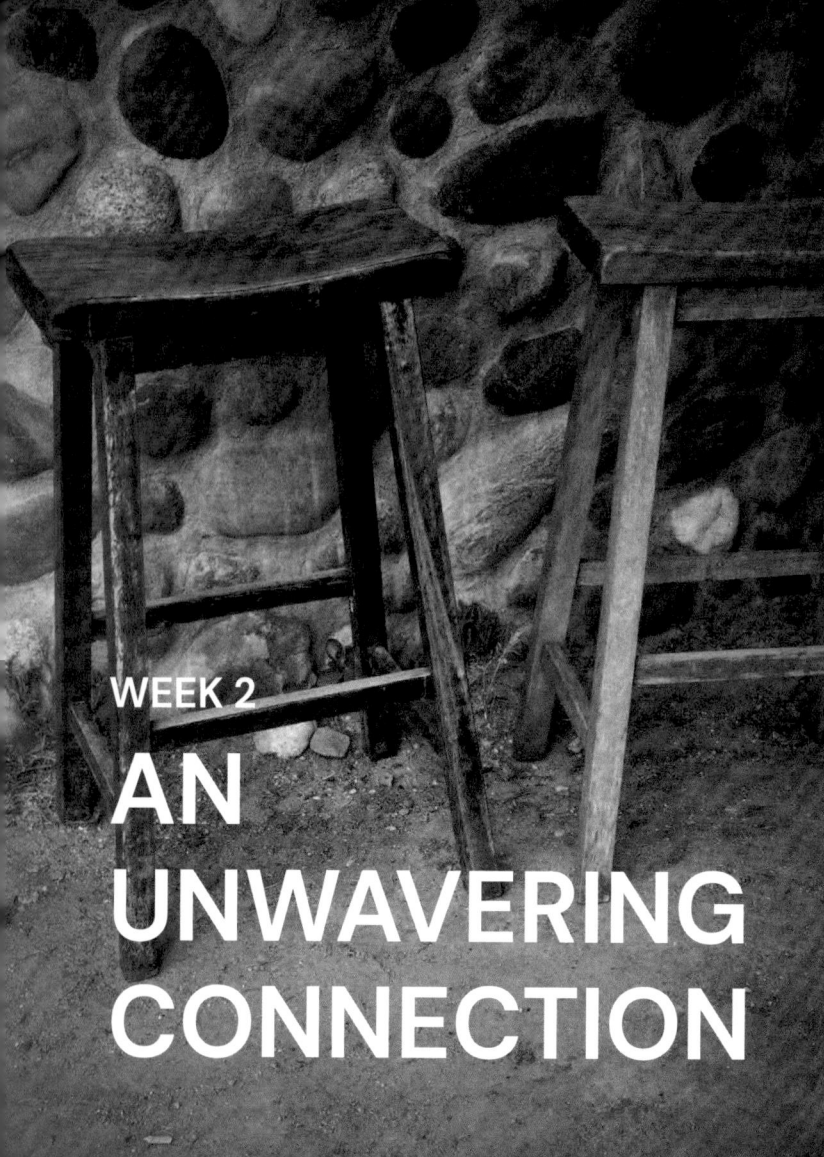

This is to my Father's glory, that you bear much fruit, showing yourselves to be my disciples.
John 15:8

2.1 PREPARATION

Several years ago, I (Steve) had a unique experience that resembles how God designed human beings to live in relationship with him. And just like every good story, this one involves a brave man, a beautiful girl, and a weak man. I'll let you figure out who's who.

I've always had a good dose of thrill-seeking in my blood. So, when my good friend Paul asked me to go skydiving, I was *ALL IN* – especially because I was a poor intern and he offered to pay.

When the big day arrived, our group of friends headed to our destination. Four of us piled into one car, including my new girlfriend. How I convinced Cheri to jump out of an airplane is still a mystery to me, so we'll just chock it up to young love.

Three people in the car were terrified, but for me, I was feeling rather macho. With my nerves at ease, I decided to liven things up. I grabbed my camcorder (before the days of smartphone cameras) and took on the role of annoying big brother. I asked many annoying questions, including, "Jim, do you have any final words to share with your parents?"

After signing our lives away, we were trained by master jumpers on how to safely jump out of an airplane. And since they had jumped hundreds of times before, we were focused intently on the precise instruction, demonstration videos, and hands-on training for every step of the process. They eventually deemed us "prepared to fly." We suited up. Off we went. When I saw the plane, it looked ancient – and it didn't add to anyone's confidence levels. Let's just say it looked more like an invention of Wilbur and Orville Wright than Elon Musk.

Up we went... 1,000... 2,000... 3,000... all the way to 13,000 feet. At this point, the fact that we were riding tandem with a master jumper harnessed behind our bodies was paramount. Quite literally, my tandem partner *had my back*. However, I had one issue with the tandem policy. It was Cheri's tandem partner. He was 6'2", well-built, and handsome. Did I mention he had an Australian accent? And if that's not bad enough, he jumped out of airplanes for a living. Come on man! Want to guess who the brave man in the story was?

When we arrived at 13,000 feet, the doors suddenly opened. Fear immediately appeared to me in full effect. All my feelings of bravado vanished. Thankfully, I'm in the back of the plane with only one person behind me, which gave me a few extra minutes to muster up some courage. I watch person after person inch their way to the edge, fearing for their life. As they take one step out the door, they scream with terror and disappear instantly. Okay, it's almost my turn.

With only one jumper behind me, I secretly wondered, "Is it too late to bail? What was I thinking?" (the weak man in the story has now been revealed). But there was one BIG PROBLEM. Guess who was behind me? Hint: she's the beautiful girl in the story.

As I looked over my shoulder, I secretly hoped to find a fearful girl who wanted to be rescued. Instead, I found an enthusiastic girl brimming with anticipation, virtually pushing me out the door. Clearly, I had passed the point of no return. Now, my manhood was on the line. It was GO TIME!

I inched up to the edge, then instinctively looked down. Bad idea. My head was spinning dizzy. My tandem partner sensed my hesitation. Just then, he tapped me on the shoulder and said, "You got this! We're in this together!" The part of me that contemplated not jumping, quickly dissipated. The next thing I remember is doing a 360-reverse spin into the free fall. Talk about sensory overload.

For 60 seconds, I zoom through the sky, free falling at one hundred feet per second. It was an exhilarating adrenaline rush that I didn't want to end. But eventually, I had to pull the parachute. Could there be anything more important than remembering that detail? Don't ask me how, but I forgot. I know, by now you're judging me. But I'm still alive, so hang with me.

Once again, the presence of my tandem connection changed everything. He reminded me of the most important thing – pull the parachute. Then, as the parachute went up, we glided downward. We rejoiced together. I immediately thanked him for making the whole experience the best thrill-seeking moment of my life. I thanked him for *having my back*. With joy, he said, "That's what I'm here for, man. You can't fly solo and still make it." Then, he points towards the picturesque landscape, with a pink sunset sky behind the rolling hills and plush green meadows below. Floating through the air, our entire friend group collectively savored the moment on our way back to solid ground. Mission accomplished!

Turns out, skydiving was an exhilarating experience – despite the fears. So I wondered, "Could this become a new hobby?" Nope. I was on an intern budget. But, even though skydiving didn't become a life hobby, it did become a life metaphor. Just as I flew in tandem through the sky on my way to a remarkable experience, we were created to live in tandem with God in route to a remarkable life.

When you're harnessed to Jesus, you will encounter a level of intimate connection that will transform who you are and how you live.

What will change? Your priorities, your perspectives, your passions, and your pursuits. When you remain connected to Christ in your life, you'll gain confidence that he'll provide the wisdom you need for every moment. You'll have assurance that he always has your back. When uncertainty scares you, he will provide the courage you need to step through the open door on your way to fulfilling the mission. And, if you ever feel like bailing, he will tap you on your shoulder to remind you that he is with you, and that you're in it together. You can't go on the journey alone. You'll never make it.

As life unfolds, God delights in reminding us what matters most. He opens doors for us to step through and directs us to look up and take in the beauty and wonder that surrounds us – to savor and enjoy life. Alongside our community, as we strive toward aligning our lives with God's mission, we will experience the joy and fulfillment for which we were made. This is no small thing, yet it's so important to the human journey.

In essence, if we are going to become true disciples of Jesus, we must choose to live in tandem with him every day as we travel through life in community with God's mission in focus. We are disciples who are learning from – and connected to – our Master, Guide, and Teacher. We are ambassadors who have a mission that requires passionate devotion and relentless courage to dig deeper than ever before. We are a tribe that moves toward our mission not just as individuals or even as a small unit, but as a movement of disciples who are collectively connected in the present – and with the generations who have gone before us.

> Those who believed the word that day numbered 3,000. They were all baptized and added *to the church*. Every believer was faithfully devoted to following the teachings of the apostles. Their hearts were mutually linked to one another, sharing communion and coming together regularly for prayer. A deep sense of holy awe swept over everyone, and the apostles performed many miraculous signs and wonders. All the believers were in fellowship as one body, and they shared with one another whatever they had. *Out of generosity* they even sold their assets to distribute the proceeds to those who were in need among them. Daily they met together in the temple courts and in one another's homes to celebrate communion. They shared meals together with joyful hearts and tender humility. They were continually filled with praises to God, enjoying the favor of all the people. And the Lord kept adding to their number daily those who were coming to life.
>
> *Acts 2:41-47*

2.2 STUDY

On one occasion, Jesus wanted to pass on a critical message to his disciples because he knew his death was near. As was often the case, Jesus used a metaphor from the earth to convey a deep, life-altering truth. Through the imagery of a vineyard, Jesus explained what was required of a disciple to "bear fruit."

Bearing fruit is the evidence of authentic transformation. It is also the evidence that you are cultivating a personal relationship with Christ and experiencing the reality of the Holy Spirit at work in your life. According to Jesus, for someone to "bear fruit," they must live in relational connection with him.

Listen to Jesus' words that describe some of the dynamics of a personal relationship with God.

> I am the True Vine, and my Father is the gardener. Every branch in me that does not bear fruit he takes away; and every branch that does bear fruit he prunes, that it may bear more fruit. I am the Vine, you are the branches.
>
> **Abide in me as I abide in you.**
>
> Just as the branch cannot bear fruit by itself unless it **abides in the vine**, neither can you unless you **abide in me.**

> I am the True Vine, you are the branches. Those who **abide in me** and **I in them** bear much fruit, because apart from me you can do nothing.
>
> **This is to my Father's glory**, that you bear much fruit, showing yourselves to be my disciples.
>
> John 15:1-2, 4-5, 8

Jesus is the *True Vine*... and we are *the branches*.

The Father tends to the vineyard. He is the Vinedresser; or he could be called the gardener or the farmer.

> When Jesus said, "I am the True Vine... and you are the branches," he was using the metaphor of fruit to describe the process of character transformation. Throughout Scripture, the concept of "fruit" is always associated with good works or character change. "Fruit" points to a thought, attitude, or action that we can embody through the power and grace of the Holy Spirit. It only happens when we are "abiding in Christ" – i.e. we are relationally connected to our Creator and rooted in our identity in him.
>
> In other words, godly character, or "good works," (that's the fruit) is produced through our lives when we (the branches) remain connected to Jesus (the True Vine).

Our job is NOT to *produce* the fruit... that's God's job.

What's our job? **To abide** (in the True Vine).

The path to experiencing God's presence is through abiding.

In John 15, Jesus used the word *abide* ten times. The word *abide* is translated from the Greek word, *meno,* which means, "to remain in," "to stay with," "to move in with," "to live with," or "to abide." When the word *meno* was used in the first century, it was a common word (not a religious word) that had relational connotations and implications. In essence, Jesus used this commonly known term to communicate the importance of remaining in continual relational connection to him – i.e. to live in tandem as we travel through life. He was showing the disciples how the process of transformation works – by remaining harnessed to the life source, Jesus Christ, and by remaining dependent on the Holy Spirit to do the work of transformation rather than trying to do it on our own.

Jesus was articulating what Paul later described as being "in Christ" and Christ being "in us." There's an intimate connection that is established and cultivated by every transformed follower of Christ. So, if you want to experience genuine life transformation, abiding in Christ must become the core pursuit of your life. It is the only path that jettisons us towards experiencing the deep work of God in our lives.

Jesus was clear: apart from an ongoing connection with Christ, real transformation will never become our reality.

Sadly, this kind of connection and transformation isn't the ethos of many professed Christians. That means that they are missing out on God's foundational vision – to be intimately and joyfully connected to their Creator, while simultaneously experiencing the fruit of the Spirit.

The Apostle Paul sheds light on the essence of transformation:

> As we are transformed to be like the Messiah, our lives are gradually becoming brighter and more beautiful as God enters our lives and we become like him.
>
> *2 Corinthians 3:18 PAR*

2.3 CHANGE

You probably don't think too much about farming, but I'm sure you know that farmers don't produce their crops. They don't make avocados or bananas. That isn't the job of the farmer. What the farmer does is cultivate environments where life has the possibility to grow. Farmers partner with nature (i.e. the sun, water, soil, etc.) to prepare a place for seeds to germinate and grow. Their tasks involve planning, hard work, and patience. Ultimately, the result of the growth (i.e. producing the fruit) is out of the farmer's control.

Similarly, when it comes to producing fruit in our lives, we can't control the outcomes of growth. However, we do have a role to play in the growth process. Like farmers, we don't produce the fruit. But that doesn't mean we refrain from all the effort, hard work, or the cultivation of an environment for growth to occur.

We can use our human efforts to manufacture or produce a wide variety of things in our lives. However, the deeper kind of transformation that we long for is never attained that way. According to the Scriptures, if we live our everyday lives depending entirely on ourselves for growth and change, we will inevitably fail to live the fruitful life Jesus envisions.

The Fuel of a Fruitful Life

To be a fruitful disciple, we must do the diligent work of cultivating an interior environment where the mystery of God's Spirit is welcomed to grow us, speak to us, and change us. This is the quiet and sometimes solo journey where one attains spiritual depth, maturity, and whole-life transformation. This is where God does his deepest work. It's where God begins to help us integrate our mind, will, emotions, and behaviors. When we put the right emphasis on the right thing (i.e. abiding in Christ), everything will begin to change – our perspectives, our priorities, our passions, and our pursuits.

Abiding in Christ is the fuel of a fruitful life. Without it, we die a slow death.

When we engage the disciple's journey with proper focus, we're reminded that God is the One who deserves the credit for fruit bearing, not us. It is for his glory, not our own. Along the way, we learn from our Master to stop seeking the spotlight. We quiet the seductive pull to have our egos stroked by how much we accomplish ourselves. We discover how to minimize our self-obsessions and recalibrate our pride, self-reliance, and over-confidence in our ability to handle life on our own. Along the way, we begin to care more about whether we reflect Jesus (and glorify him), rather than whether we are reflecting a particular image of ourselves to others.

I'm going to keep it real with you: there have been many times when I've allowed myself to remain disconnected from God. I get distracted. My wife can attest to this if needed. Can you relate? Or sometimes, I just lose my way and wander. I lose focus on the cultivation of intimacy with God. In some seasons, I have felt as if I was like a large tree that's rotting from the inside and no longer growing. Why? Because I'm a disconnected branch and the source of life isn't flowing in and through me. I start to live on my own. I live for myself and in my own strength. This is a trap that I have fallen into more than once. Maybe you have too.

Even as disciples who understand the truths in John 15, we can quickly fall into allowing our insides to rot because we aren't truly abiding in the Vine. We've all been there. We get distracted by someone or something. Maybe we get swept up into all the activity around us and lose sight of what it means to abide. We wander. Or, maybe we lose sight of our once established priority to stay continually connected to God. We forget that this quest is ultimately the path to stay on if we want to become healthy and whole again.

To be a healthy and whole person, you need to stop frantically running through life without focusing on what is most essential.

The most important thing about your life as a disciple is your personal relationship with Jesus Christ. There is absolutely nothing more essential to your journey through life. In other words, prayer is the path into encountering the presence of God.

For me, it's helpful to identify the things that distract me the most. I've learned how critical it is to remain intentional about leaving those distractions behind. When I don't, what I tend to do is pretend. It's the truth. Sometimes I pretend on the outside, so people don't really know how distant I am with God on the inside. In essence, it's like I start attaching "fruit" to my branches with scotch tape so it looks like fruit is really growing from my tree. But it's not, and deep down, I know it. This happens when I allow myself to focus on lesser things – like how I'm perceived by others. I find myself trying to control what people think about me. I even tell these little white lies to protect a certain image I want to portray.

Have you ever been consumed with producing for other people? Have you ever tried to project a particular image of yourself or your life? I think it's safe to say that if we reach that point, there's something unhealthy in our souls – and we must face that.

We've all been there. And we'll probably be there again. But, if we keep zeroing in on what things look like on the surface rather than what's really going on underneath the surface, our soul will wither because we (the branch) will be disconnected from the source of life (the True Vine). We can pretend for a season, but it always catches up to us. Maybe we can even get good at it and make it last longer. But we know what's going on and it's not good for the soul.

At some point, we must face the reality that we were not designed to pretend, nor were we created to live self-contained and self-reliant.

To be human means that we must learn to overcome the temptation to attach ourselves to earthly things rather than to heavenly things. This is the path to finding the life and meaning that we're searching for. It isn't always easy. But every time we attach the deeper part of ourselves to anything but God, we choose to cease abiding in him. If we try to find our worth and value in something or someone else, it won't last. If we find our identity in an accomplishment or certain status, at some point it will come tumbling down. We'll be left empty.

However, if we abide, we are reminded of our true identity in Christ. We remember that we are loved. We begin to experience love, joy, peace, goodness... the fruit of the Spirit. When we are truly abiding in Christ, we are deriving our worth and value *from Christ.* We're connected to our source of life. His Spirit is flowing, and our soul is not only centered in Christ, but we are also deeply and intimately connected to God's unchanging, unconditional love.

We will all have moments when we realize that we have drifted away from God or lost our focus. This is part of being human. If you don't think that can happen to you, you might just need a new infusion of humility. We must reckon with this reality: one of the greatest enemies to abiding in Christ is buying into the lie that we already are. We can easily mistake light bulbs for the sun if all we're doing is looking for some version of light – but they are altogether different. If you want to have a healthy soul, it will be directly impacted by the strength of your connection to the True Vine. A branch that isn't connected will eventually wither and die.

When abiding is a reality in your life, your soul will become vibrant and alive. Godly fruit will emerge, and you will be living more and more into the abundant, joy-filled life that God designed you to live. You will find peace, only to be found in Christ alone.

> "God can't give us peace and happiness apart from Himself because there is no such thing." – *C.S. Lewis*

2.4 ACTION

What happens when you abide in Christ?

If we don't make it a priority to pursue transformation into Christ-likeness, then we are just going to continue to produce Christians who are indistinguishable in their character from so many non-Christians. This is one of many reasons that makes abiding in Christ so essential.

A human being cannot consistently abide in Christ and continue to be proud, rude, judgmental, hypocritical, self-obsessed, exclusive, and loveless. Yet, haven't we all met Christians who are some of those things – maybe all of them? Sure. So let's dig deeper to uncover why that is the case.

When we're not abiding, our soul begins to shrivel over time. We may not detect it, but we are disconnected from God. As a result, we don't live with the power of God flowing within us. In contrast, when we are truly abiding, we experience an abundance of things – a life of joy, grace, gratitude, peace, patience, kindness, courage, goodness, and so much more. Most of all, you will experience the love of God.

In Galatians 5:22-23, we find a list of godly virtues which are described as the "fruit of the Spirit." In the larger context of this passage, Paul articulates the dark reality of sinful living, describing it as, "living in the flesh." He's warning us of the great danger of allowing the cravings of the self to rule our hearts.

In contrast, Paul goes on to highlight the role of the Holy Spirit in our lives with the language of "living in the Spirit." In essence he says, it's only by the grace and power of the Holy Spirit that we experience true life change. Paul goes on to tell us that the only way to overcome temptation is by living a "Spirit-led" and "Spirit-filled" life. He's telling us that we can't live a fruitful life on our own, but only by the Spirit who fills us up, leads us, and ultimately empowers us to live like Christ. We cannot be overcomers in our own strength.

As Jesus' disciples, we must learn to depend less on self (the flesh) and more on the Holy Spirit. As a result, godly virtues will be reflected in our lives. We will exemplify Christ-like character traits, not because we are trying harder or giving more effort to "be like Christ." Rather, we begin to experience real transformation as a result of abiding in the True Vine. We do our part (abiding), and then God does his part (transforming). Abiding involves pursuing closeness with God, meaning we communicate with him, we share with him what's going on in our hearts, and we do our best to listen and try to understand what God is saying to us. We are communing with our Creator. We are drawing near to him. And as we draw closer to God, he promises to draw closer to us (James 4:8). Without proximity to God and intimacy with God, transformation comes to a screeching halt.

Self-Assessment

Let's take a few moments to identify the fruit in our lives. This will help us pinpoint where we have potential for growth. Below is a self-assessment of the fruit of the Spirit with a list of the fruit from Galatians 5:22-23. In the broader passage, notice that the Apostle Paul says that we are to actively engage in putting off sin (resisting the flesh) and putting on the fruit of the Spirit (through a Spirit-led, Spirit-empowered life).

2.4 Action

As you look in the metaphorical mirror to assess yourself, consider each fruit listed below. When you assess the joy that you are experiencing in your life, how evident is it? Maybe there's a mild amount? Or perhaps you see more joy and let's call it *medium*. Or you might even say that you feel deep joy and exude it in your life right now - we'll call that *hot!* Again, look at each of the fruit along with the descriptions and questions, to assess whether you're mild, medium, or hot when it comes to that particular fruit. Just remember that you are a work in progress. We all are! So the goal here is to cultivate the ongoing process of transformation in your life by first doing some honest self-reflection.

Love: Love is about being selfless, even sacrificial. How are you embodying selflessness? How compassionate has your heart been this week – toward a hurting person, someone in need, or a friend who just needed a listening ear? Do you notice when the people in your life are struggling with something, hurting, or when something is not quite right with them? How tender is your heart toward people far from God, and what action have you been taking to reach out to them and/or serve them? At any point in the last week, did you take on the spirit of the Pharisees – i.e. have you reflected a critical, judgmental, prideful, or boastful spirit? Did you really listen to people and remain present with them when they were talking? Did you ask questions to show people that you care about them and value them?

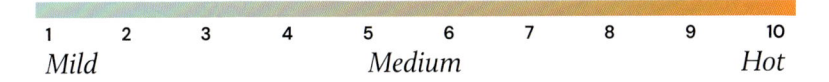

1	2	3	4	5	6	7	8	9	10
Mild				Medium					Hot

Joy: Joy involves experiencing a deep, residing delight internally that is revealed in various ways externally. How often do you complain versus express gratitude? Do you recall any moments of laughter or fun in the last two weeks? Was there any moment when something didn't go your way, yet you maintained joy in the midst of a difficult situation or unwanted circumstance? Do you find yourself rationalizing your deficit of joy even now? Are you moody? How often do you feel discouraged? Are you a pessimistic or critical person? If you are, why do you think that is? Do you recognize a joy inside of you that gives you strength and optimism for each day?

1	2	3	4	5	6	7	8	9	10
Mild				*Medium*					*Hot*

Peace: During the last week, to what degree did you feel consistently at rest in your heart and mind with God? How much have you been worrying lately? How much anxiety are you experiencing this week? To what degree are your worries, anxieties, and fears affecting your inner peace? Did you experience more contentment or discontentment this week? Are you restless and/or discontented? Would others consider you argumentative? Do you feel internal chaos or feel overwhelmed on a regular basis? Are you a promoter of peace and harmony in your relationships? Do you consider yourself a centered person?

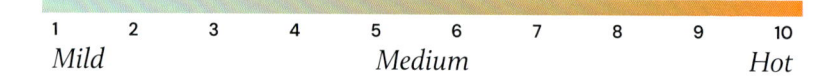

1	2	3	4	5	6	7	8	9	10
Mild				*Medium*					*Hot*

Patience: What is your response when things don't go your way? Are you capable of waiting gracefully and restfully when something is going slower than you'd like (i.e. the grocery store line, traffic, with your children or roommate, etc.)? Are you patient with people who don't finish a task as quickly as you expected (at school, at work, at home, etc.)? Are you consistently

2.4 Action

irritable? Do you regularly find yourself in a hurry or rushing to the next thing? Why is that?

1	2	3	4	5	6	7	8	9	10
Mild				Medium					Hot

Kindness: Are you postured to lend a helping hand, even when you are very busy? Do you consistently offer encouraging words to people in your life and affirm what's good about them? Are you tender-hearted towards others? Do you have any prejudices that cause you to be unkind? Are you a sarcastic or cunning person? Is there a cruel or mean streak in you? Do you genuinely care about people, and express that to them? Are you considered rude by any of your friends?

1	2	3	4	5	6	7	8	9	10
Mild				Medium					Hot

Goodness: Over the last two weeks, how often did you do something out of the goodness of your heart? Is your day-to-day life making the people around you better? Do you feel your heart growing or shrinking when it comes to generosity (this includes the giving of your financial resources, your time to others, etc.)? Are you consistently seeking to be generous and servant-hearted with your talents, time, and treasures? Are you more of a spiritual contributor than a spiritual consumer? How willing are you to serve someone, even when you know you won't be acknowledged or affirmed for it?

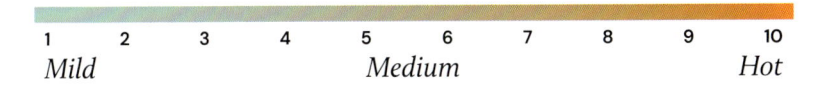

1	2	3	4	5	6	7	8	9	10
Mild				Medium					Hot

Faithfulness: Would the people that you live and work with describe you as a dependable and responsible person? According to the people you are closest to in your life, are you consistently a person of your word? Do you procrastinate? Do you forget to do what you said you would, or do you follow through consistently? Do you show up to things you're supposed to be at? Do you faithfully use your talents and spiritual gifts to serve others? Do you seek to know God's Word and apply it to your life on a daily basis? Are you a loyal employee who can be entrusted with a project, person, or task? Can people *really* count on you? Are you reliable?

1	2	3	4	5	6	7	8	9	10
Mild				*Medium*					*Hot*

Gentleness: When you share truth with someone, do you also extend tenderness and empathy? How frequently and quickly do you become angry with people? Do you have a tendency to criticize people with your words or tear them down with sarcasm? Do you listen with genuine care for others and respond to what they are saying with sincerity and concern? Do you have a tendency to be harsh? Do you find yourself showing empathy for people who are hurting, lonely, or in need of some comfort? Over the last two weeks, has your heart been more tender and soft? Or, has it been a little cold and callous?

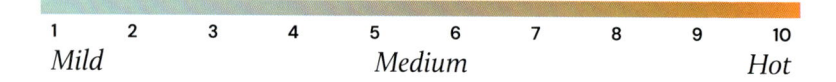

1	2	3	4	5	6	7	8	9	10
Mild				*Medium*					*Hot*

Self-Control: Are there any bad habits that you can't shake that have been troubling you? Do you ever find yourself saying things you wish you would not have said? Would those who know you well consider you to be impulsive, or semi-impulsive? How often do you experience what the Apostle Paul speaks about in Romans 7 (i.e. I do what I don't want to do. I don't do what I want to do.)? Do you ever find yourself saying things in anger that you know you should never have said? When things get heated, do you have a hard time holding your tongue? How often do your emotions "get the best of you?"

1	2	3	4	5	6	7	8	9	10
Mild				Medium					Hot

Now, let's look at your results. Identify which virtues are most evident in your life. Go ahead and circle two or three of them. These would be the ones you assessed as the hottest.

Love   Joy   Peace   Patience   Kindness   Goodness
Faithfulness   Gentleness   Self-control

On the flip side, which virtues are not as evident and in need of God's transforming work? Go ahead and circle two or three of them. This would be the ones you assessed as the *mildest.*

Love   Joy   Peace   Patience   Kindness   Goodness
Faithfulness   Gentleness   Self-control

A Simple Prayer

Now, take a few minutes to pray through the fruit of the Spirit. You can pray out loud or silently. You could even write out your prayer, a spiritual practice that helps me focus. It also allows me to look back later to see what I prayed about and how God answered those prayers. However you choose to pray, express your desire for transformation in each of the fruit of the Spirit. Ask God to show you how to grow in the fruit that isn't as evident. In other words, what do you need to *put on...* or *put off*? And remember, this journey isn't to be done by your own strength. Yes, you have an active role, but your role starts with abiding in Christ. Then, remain intentional in how you engage life in regard to these virtues, relying on God's grace and power to change you. Invite the Holy Spirit to reveal any action steps that you need to take to do your part in the growth process. As you pray through the Christ-like virtues in Galatians 5:22-23, zero in on the ones you desire to be more evident in your life in this next season. Pay close attention to what God's Spirit is showing you and saying to you.

2.5 COMMUNITY

After you share a meal together, take some time to read through a few of these scenarios one at a time. Discuss how the fruit of the Spirit may play out. In other words, discuss how you could bear fruit despite the challenges of the situation described. What would it look like in these situations if someone was bearing fruit? Be honest about how *you* might respond in the given scenario (perhaps in the right way, or maybe in the wrong way). The goal of these discussions is to gain insights into what fruit-bearing looks like in real life scenarios. If you want, you can describe your own scenario and ask the group to weigh in on how they could/would respond, or even to give you feedback on how you could respond better the next time you're in a similar situation.

Scenario 1
Someone at work says something that hurts your feelings. It makes you angry. Your initial impulse is to get them back with a cunning, sarcastic, or unkind comment. But you know that isn't the Christ-like way to respond. You know that you need to put off your fleshly desire and put on godly virtue. What if you stopped and asked yourself, "What does self-control, patience, kindness, and goodness look like in this moment?" How can you be gentle to someone who doesn't seem to deserve gentleness? What does godly strength and spiritual maturity look like in how you respond?

Scenario 2
You have a packed schedule one day. You are feeling a ton of pressure. You are stressed out. Plus, you feel rushed and hurried

as a deadline approaches. Then, one of your co-workers reveals that they are going through something really painful. You can tell that they want/need someone to talk to, however, you don't have time to extend care and concern for them right now. What shall you do? Perhaps in that moment, you ask yourself, "How can I embody kindness and love in this moment? What should I say or do? Can I meet this person's needs, and will I trust God to help me still achieve what I need to achieve? How do I communicate with love, kindness, goodness, and gentleness?" Or maybe, you engage with them in a godly way, but you kindly tell them where you're at and what you're dealing with. Discuss and analyze possibilities. How do you honor God and them in light of your own personal challenges?

Scenario 3

You find yourself talking negatively and/or critically about someone or something in your life. You know that you are complaining and grumbling. Or, maybe you are harboring an unhealthy emotion like resentment or bitterness. Stop and ask yourself, "How can I cultivate gratitude and joy about my life and the people in my life, even when everything doesn't go my way? How can I shift my perspective to align with God's?" What are things you could do to foster joy and gratitude, despite things not going well right now?

Scenario 4

You find yourself anxious and irritable. Stop and ask yourself, "How can I trust God with what I am anxious about, so I can experience God's peace? How do I embody patience and kindness so that I become less irritable? Why am I irritable? And what does God have to say about my irritable and/or anxious spirit? What fruit am I in need of bearing?"

Scenario 5

You gave someone your word that you would finish a project or do something for them. But in reality, you have reasons why you don't think you can pull it off, or don't want to pull it off. You want to be a person of your word, but you find yourself between a rock and a hard place, not knowing what to do. Perhaps you can stop and ask God, "What does it mean to be faithful even when I don't feel like it? What does it mean to practice goodness, even when it's easier not to?" What is God's best for you in this moment?

Life Application

To close out your community time, invite every person in the group to share one application (or specific next step) that they will take this week in response to the discussion. After each person shares, close your time in prayer for one another. Have each person pray for the person to their right or left. Or, have one person pray for the whole group.

2.6 FOCUS

Before this week comes to a close, let's go back to John 15, where we find the concept of pruning.

> He cuts off every branch in me that bears no fruit, while every branch that does bear fruit he prunes so that it will be even more fruitful. You are already clean because of the words I have spoken to you.
>
> *John 15:2-3*

If you observe the pruning process at a vineyard, it looks like a disaster. The gardener looks like he's attacking the plant. There are beautiful things all over the ground that look like they should not have been cut off. You may think, "What a waste!" But a skilled gardener understands that everything taken off needs to be taken off so that the vine can reach its fruit-bearing potential.

Jesus is telling us that when the knife comes into your life, things need to get cut off and put to death. Sometimes they are things that you think should stay. It may feel like something is being wasted – but Jesus tells us that it needs to be pruned and cut off. Why? So he can bring life out of death; so that more abundant fruit can spring forth.

What's one example of something in your life that God has pruned, cut off, or put to death?

Maybe you've been bearing fruit (doing what you can to serve God, extending God's love to others, showing compassion to those in need, stepping out in courage, making wise decisions, etc.) but you keep getting knocked down, or set back. Maybe you've secretly wondered where God is, or why he's not blessing you or protecting you from pain. Or, perhaps you've wondered if God is punishing you. Consider that God might be pruning you, doing the necessary work to help you become more fully human and whole once again. After all, authentic character transformation never comes without cost.

Take a moment to reflect on what it means to be pruned. Think about how God might be pruning you right now, or how God has pruned you in the past.

Pay close attention to what you think God is using to prune you.

For example, tragedy or heartbreak, illness or injury, a difficult trial or feeling of failure, a fractured relationship or broken dream, or maybe just an unpleasant season of life or time of waiting. Go ahead and jot down a few thoughts.

It does our soul good to remember that when we go through difficult things in life, there's fruit on the other side. We all know someone who has been through something very difficult, yet comes out as a better human being. We've heard people say, "I wouldn't change a thing. It wasn't easy, but now I see how God shaped and transformed me through it." What remains difficult is that we aren't privy to understand all the dynamics that go into the challenges of life. When we are going through something difficult, it's hard to see the bigger picture. But, we can be certain that God is at work in whatever is happening in our lives. In fact, he uses it as part of the pruning process.

> So we are convinced that every detail of our lives is continually woven together for good, for we are his lovers who have been called to fulfill his designed purpose.
>
> *Romans 8:28*

When we're likened to a branch, God is the Gardener who is tending to the branches. He produces the fruit as we remain connected to him through all the ups and downs of life. In the end, when we embody the fruit of the Spirit, we're given a sure sign that our character has been transformed.

When our deepest attitudes and dispositions begin to resemble Jesus', it's a result of our learning to let the Holy Spirit cultivate his life and character in us.

> "In spiritual formation we are aiming at a character and life that is so shaped that the deeds of Christ routinely and easily come from what is inside." – Dallas Willard

God desires to make us new. He longs to restore our humanity.

When he thinks about you, God wants to make a whole disciple out of a broken person.

> Stop imitating the ideals and opinions of the culture around you, but be inwardly transformed by the Holy Spirit through a total reformation of how you

think. This will empower you to discern God's will as you live a beautiful life, satisfying and perfect in his eyes.

Romans 12:2

2.7 REST

Today, we simply invite you to rest in God.

As you read this passage, do it slowly and deliberately. Invite God's Spirit to speak to you today. Receive what God wants to give you. Then, rest in gratitude for all the work that God has done, is doing, and will continue to do in your life.

Galatians 5:16–26

16-18 As you yield freely and fully to the dynamic life and power of the Holy Spirit, you will abandon the cravings of your self-life. For your self-life craves the things that offend the Holy Spirit *and hinder him from living free within you*! And the Holy Spirit's intense cravings hinder your old self-life from dominating you! So then, the two incompatible and conflicting forces within you are your self-life of the flesh and the new creation life of the Spirit. But when you are brought into the full freedom of the Spirit of grace, you will no longer be living under the domination of the law, *but soaring above it*!

19-21 The cravings of the self-life are obvious: sexual immorality, lustful thoughts, pornography, chasing after things instead of God, manipulating others, hatred of those who get in your way, senseless arguments, resentment when others are favored, temper tantrums, angry quarrels, only thinking of yourself, being in love with your own opinions, being envious of the blessings of others, murder, uncontrolled addictions, wild parties, and all other similar behavior. Haven't I already warned you that those who use their "freedom" for these things will not inherit the kingdom realm of God!

22-23 But the fruit produced by the Holy Spirit within you is divine love in all its varied expressions:
joy *that overflows*,
peace *that subdues*,
patience *that endures*,
kindness *in action*,
a life full of virtue,
faith *that prevails*,
gentleness *of heart*, and
strength *of spirit*.

Never set the law above these qualities, for they are meant to be limitless.

24-26 Keep in mind that we who belong to Jesus, the Anointed One, have already experienced crucifixion. For everything connected with our self-life was put to death on the cross and crucified with Messiah. We must live in the Holy Spirit and follow after him. So may we never be arrogant, or look down on another, *for each of us is an original*. We must forsake all jealousy that diminishes the value of others.

WEEK 3

AN UNCOMMON PURSUIT

Anyone who says, "I live in intimacy with Him," should walk the path Jesus walked.
1 John 2:6

3.1 PREPARATION

When my son Hudson began to play basketball, I (Steve) needed to teach him the fundamentals. Shooting a basketball is one essential skill. Coincidentally, I ran across a collection of films known as Master Class. This collection features various experts who have a series of videos you can learn from. One of the experts was Steph Curry, the greatest three-point shooter of all time. And since I wanted to teach my son how to shoot a basketball, I was eager to learn from the best. As a fan of basketball and a former high school player, I had some basketball knowledge, but now, I had unique access to Curry's incredible wisdom, knowledge, and perspective. This would without question increase my coaching competence. I saw this as an amazing opportunity to learn from the master shooter, in hopes that I could pass on what I was learning to my son and accelerate his development. Over a few weeks, I proceeded to learn Steph Curry's habits, disciplines, and techniques that contributed to his development in shooting and scoring. It was fascinating, helpful, and downright inspiring.

In addition, I continued to learn from other films in this collection. I watched films from world-renowned chef Gordon Ramsey on cooking, best-selling and award-winning author Malcolm Gladwell on writing, Judy Blume on storytelling, and Oscar-winning, legendary filmmaker Martin Scorsese on filmmaking. The knowledge and wisdom made available through these films is a remarkable resource for learning.

One day, I was watching a film session with Stephen Curry, and something stood out to me. I began to think about our approach to discipleship in the church. As I engaged with these films, I was acquiring an extraordinary amount of knowledge. That was so good. But I was also reminded that knowledge alone doesn't produce growth, nor does it automatically lead to proficiency or success. One can attain an immense amount of knowledge but fail to grow or change.

In its simplest form, acquiring knowledge alone (from an expert, author, mentor, etc.) can become the end goal of our learning, rather than the application of that knowledge.

If we only focus on gaining knowledge, we fill our minds with information. But if we focus on application, we fill our lives with transformation.

Discipleship must never be reduced to being students who gather more knowledge, even if it is knowledge of the Bible. For us to experience real transformation, we are to become apprentices who consistently learn and apply the knowledge we're gaining.

For a moment, just imagine something with me.

What if Steph Curry showed up at my front door and invited my son Hudson to the gym? After Hudson got over being star struck, imagine that Steph Curry took time to build a relationship with him as he spent the day together coaching him one-on-one. What if this continued day after day? As a kid who loves basketball and wants to improve his game, Hudson would be dialed in! He would become the student, the pupil, and ultimately the apprentice who is learning from a master. He'd be receptive to coaching, guidance, instruction, correction, and training on how to play basketball at the highest level. Imagine this going on for months, and eventually years. For a kid who wants to become a better basketball player, could there be any better development opportunity?

Okay, now back to reality.

I'm using my imagination because this idea resembles the discipleship process in the New Testament. A rabbi comes alongside an apprentice with hopes of developing him (or her) in the context of a relationship. He isn't focused on classroom learning, nor is he focused on gaining knowledge alone.

The focus is on how to live differently by applying what is being learned.

In today's church, we often confuse the gathering of information with the reality of formation. In the first century rabbi-disciple relationship, there was focused intentionality, an enormous commitment of time, and an immense amount of teaching and training. Yes, there was information involved; however, they understood the difference before information and application.

Jesus invites you to not simply be a student who sits in a classroom and gathers information, he invites you to enter into a personal relationship with him, to become his apprentice, and to learn how to apply what you're learning and experiencing. And though the mechanics of this apprenticeship are different in our day, the priorities remain the same. Jesus doesn't just want to spend a few minutes with you each morning. He desires to live life with you, traveling through each day together. Jesus doesn't want your discipleship to be reduced to a classroom. He wants you to encounter him in your day-to-day life. Along the way, he wants to teach and train you how to live an entirely new way, but he wants to do it in the context of a relationship. If you don't have a teacher who guides you and relates to you, then you don't have an authentic disciple. Ultimately, Jesus' desire is that you would learn from him how to live just like he would live if he was living in your place. Disciples of Jesus are God-taught, God-guided, and God-inspired.

3.2 STUDY

In the first century, to become a disciple was synonymous with becoming an apprentice. Yet, do a quick scan of modern-day Christianity, and it's hard to find people who are familiar with the apprenticeship model of the New Testament. In my experience, there aren't too many people in our today's world who embody the apprenticeship model as a way of living. Yet, that's the discipleship model that we see in the New Testament.

What is an Apprentice?

The Greek word for disciple is **mathetes,** which is used 269 times in the New Testament. This term can be translated, "*student, pupil,* or *learner.*" I think that the best English translation is *apprentice.*

An apprentice in the first century was someone who chose to be with his (or her) master under certain conditions so that he (or she) could learn from them how to live. The goal of the apprentice was to become just like their master. Over time, the apprentice would take on new habits, skills, and perspectives – all of which they had learned from their master. The core focus wasn't primarily on acquiring knowledge, rather, the apprentice would wake up each day with the intention in their heart to live in close relational proximity with their master so that they could eventually be just like him. They knew that if they were to learn how to live like their master, they had to be in relational proximity as much as possible. Notice the importance of living in tandem connection.

In the Old Testament, there's a different word for disciple. It's the word, *talmid,* which is a Hebrew term that can mean, "one who sought to become like his master." It can also mean "taught one." Embedded into the meaning of this word is a strong emphasis on the personal *relationship* between a rabbi and his disciple (or apprentice). This makes sense because disciples who want to *become just like their master* understand that close relationship is essential. Often, discipleship can be focused on what we are doing (for God). But **the most essential thing in your life as a disciple of Jesus is not what you do but who you become. God is far less interested in what you are doing for him, and much more interested in who you are becoming.**

> "Discipleship is the process of becoming who Jesus would be if he were you." – Dallas Willard

From the moment his day began, to the moment he fell asleep, the *talmid* was obsessed with learning how to live like his rabbi in all aspects of life. That didn't mean he had to change his personality, but it did mean he would make significant adjustments in his way of living. This involved reordering his priorities, reconsidering his perspectives, recalibrating his passions, and refining his pursuits. In the context of the apprentice/master relationship, his focus, mindset, and values would be reshaped and remolded. His life was all about being conformed to the image of his rabbi.

The chief goal of the Christian life could be summarized like this: We are to be conformed to the image of Christ for the glory of God and for the sake of others.

How Jesus Impacts Our Decisions

In everyday living, the ***talmid*** wanted to know precisely how his rabbi made decisions in particular situations. This was because he wanted to know how to make decisions when a similar situation arose in his life. So he would watch how his rabbi treated his friends and his enemies, how he responded to criticism and praise, how he interacted with people who disagreed with him, and how he listened to others who shared one of their struggles or how they were hurting. Apprentices would listen to how their master prayed, paid attention to his thinking processes, and discovered what he valued most and believed in at his core. This way of living shaped who the *talmid* was becoming. Over time, the apprentice would develop similar instincts, as well as embody like-minded attitudes and resemble his rabbi's behaviors. As the saying goes, more is caught than taught. And once again, that's where you find the real impact of an apprenticeship. It's rooted in close and intentional relationship. And it beckons us once again to live intimately connected to Christ, with a passionate focus on becoming like him. When Jesus invited us to follow him, he was inviting us to make a pilgrimage into the heart and life of God.

In first-century Jewish culture, a unique blessing was often used that beautifully expressed the total devotion of a disciple who consistently remained in the presence of the one he followed. The blessing would be:

May you always be covered by the dust of your rabbi.

In other words, may you follow him so closely that the dust of his feet will kick up from the ground and cover your clothing, your feet, and your face. The dustier you got, the better. As much as possible, a disciple wanted to keep his rabbi in sight because it allowed him to watch closely as he discovered how to live in this new way of his rabbi. He sought to be harnessed to him as much as possible, and to be as near to him as he could.

Imitation as a Result of Admiration

In Capernaum during the first century, rabbis would be seen walking in and out of town with a crew of disciples following behind. If a rabbi bent down to smell a flower, his disciples would do the same. If he grabbed a stick to chew on, the disciples would also grab a stick to chew on. When a rabbi ate a meal, the apprentice would pay attention to how he prayed and even to what he ate and how slowly or swiftly he ate.

Simply put, these disciples learned everything from their rabbis, and then sought to adopt new habits, attitudes, and behaviors. They learned their stories and observed how they interacted with their families. They noticed how the rabbi lived out his mission and emulated how their rabbi honored the Sabbath. And of course, they sat at the feet of their rabbi when they taught a lesson or expounded on the Hebrew Scriptures. In essence, these disciples did anything and everything to conform to the image of their rabbi.

Ultimately, what mattered most to a disciple wasn't the particular activity their rabbi was doing. What *really mattered* to a disciple was *being with* his rabbi, doing whatever he was doing, learning how to live just like him in every way. In our day, the concept of having faith in Christ has become completely isolated from being Jesus' apprentice and discovering how to do what he said and did.

For the disciple, every activity of life was an opportunity to learn from his rabbi how to be just like him.

3.3 CHANGE

Have you ever wanted to know God's will for your life? Haven't we all? Today, let's get some clarity.

In Romans 8:28-29 we read:

> And we know that in all things God works for the good of those who love him, who have been called according to his purpose. For those God foreknew he also predestined to be conformed to the image of his Son…

Let's zero in on a few things. First, *in all things God works*. That's great news. God is working in your life in all areas. Second, not only does God work, he *works for the good of those who love him and who have been called according to his purpose.* That's more great news if you love God and are called into his purpose – and you are. Go a little further and you'll notice that God knows things in advance. Recognize that God foreknew your step of faith in Jesus Christ, and that he knew he was going to conform you into the likeness of Jesus. So, if you want to know God's will for your life, there it is – that you would be conformed into the image of Jesus Christ. God wants to mold you into looking just like Jesus more and more every single day.

It took us just two verses to uncover the essence of God's will for your life. You're welcome!

Okay, okay, but isn't there more to it? Maybe that's just not satisfactory to you. And I get where you're coming from. But here's the thing: I know we often want to know more specifics. We want more clarity. God, just tell me what grad school to go to, who to marry, where to live, what degree path to pursue, what job to choose, etc. But the truth is, God is far more interested in making sure you don't look like the world. His passion for your life is to help you discover how to look more and more like your Savior – no matter where you live, no matter what school you go to, no matter who you marry.

God's plan for your life is to shape you into his likeness.

I Will Not Conform

Let's zoom in on the word "conform." In Romans, Paul tells us not to be conformed to the world (12:2). But he also tells us to be conformed to the image of Jesus (8:29). At a base level, know that we are going to be conformed into something. There's no neutral in life. In other words, your thoughts are leading you toward God or toward yourself. And the result of those thoughts will either conform you to the world or conform you to the likeness of Christ.

These two words tell an interesting story. And to fully understand these two words (and how they impact our lives), we have to dig deeper into the original Greek language to understand the nuances and dynamics about these words. Why? Well, for starters, in English we read it as the same word: conform. But these two words are vastly different in meaning.

In Romans 12:2, we read Paul telling us not to conform. Understanding the definition of the Greek word used here can give us a valuable insight.

The Greek word that Paul uses in Romans 12:2 means, "assuming a similar outward form by following the same pattern, model, or mold." One way to think about this word is to think about Jell-O. If you want it to be shaped like a heart, then you can put in the Jell-O and make it a heart. If you want to make a Christmas tree, that works too. Just put it into the mold, let it chill for a bit, and there you have it. In essence, the word conform in this text means that you become whatever shape you are put into.

Now, go back to Romans 8 where we get a different Greek word. Once again, we read the same word conform, but here's what this word means: Paul tells us that we are shaped or molded by "sharing the same inner essence or identity; showing similar behavior from having the same essential nature." So, when we are conforming to the world, it's something like Jell-O. We are being poured into a mold and taking on the shape of that mold. You might think you are neutral, but along the way you are being poured into the mold of the world. But in Romans 8, there's a stark contrast. When we are being conformed into the likeness of Jesus, we are actively cultivating a relationship with him whereby we're now united with Christ. We begin to take on the very life of Christ through the work and power of the Holy Spirit. We begin to share an inner essence and have a new identity. As a result, we are being changed from the inside out into the very life and character of Christ by the work of the Spirit.

The world wants to squeeze us into its mold. The world tries to conform us from the outside in – but Jesus Christ wants to transform us from the inside out, shaping us into his likeness. He wants us to be united with him, to receive a new identity, and to become something altogether new.

All of this means that who we become depends on where we fix our eyes and where we set our minds. The Scriptures tell us to "fix our eyes on Jesus, the Author and Perfecter of our faith"

(Hebrews 12:2). And we are to "set our mind on things above" (Colossians 3:2).

In Romans 8:5, Paul tells us:

> Those who live according to the flesh have their minds set on what the flesh desires; but those who live in accordance with the Spirit have their minds set on what the Spirit desires.

What is your mindset? In your everyday, ordinary life, what is your mind set on? Is it set on the flesh – what you want, what you think and how you can remain in control? Or, is your mind set on the Spirit – what does God want? What does God think? How can God be the one in control of your life?

I love what Paul says next in verse 6:

> "For the mind set on the flesh is death, but the mind set on the Spirit is life and peace..."

The truth in this verse has enormous implications for our lives. If you choose a mindset that is focused on you, or on living *in the flesh*, the result is going to be death. But if you set your mind on the Spirit, you'll experience life and peace. In other words, there are things that will emerge from within you that will be life to you and for you. You'll also experience something we're all looking for more of – peace. And those things will live on. They'll have meaning in both the present life and the life to come.

Jesus is far more interested in who you are becoming than in what you are doing.

3.4 ACTION

Everything that Jesus teaches us to do, he himself put into daily practice in circumstances just like ours. We become like him by following him in the ways that he chose to live himself. The gospels give us detailed biographical accounts to help us get to know Jesus. As disciples, we learn to immerse ourselves in who Jesus was and understand how he lived so that we can become just like him. We grasp his teachings in ever deepening ways – and we apply them to our lives in his strength and by his power at work within us. Doing these things are essential if we're going to become fully devoted apprentices of Jesus. Once again, the goal is for our whole life to be increasingly oriented in the way that Jesus' life was so that we can be conformed to his image. This is what it means to "grow in the grace and knowledge of Christ" (2 Peter 3:18).

We are not only saved by grace, we live by grace.

That means that every activity in which we engage can be approached and thought about in a whole new way. Life becomes a gift to us as we invite the abounding grace of God to pervade every aspect of our lives.

Jesus Isn't Interested in Religion

Life with Jesus isn't to be compartmentalized as if we think of our "spiritual life" as different from our real life. Christianity isn't just the religion we're part of. God designed you as a holistic being, and he wants you to integrate him into every aspect of how you live. To have the opportunity to learn how to live from

Jesus in this way is the greatest opportunity any human being can have.

Here's a beautiful picture of grace that's painted with words. It's a snapshot into understanding what a transformed life looks like – one that's permeated with grace not only for salvation but for all of life.

> Now God has us where he wants us, with all the time in this world and the next to shower grace and kindness upon us in Christ Jesus. Saving is all his idea, and all his work. All we do is trust him enough to let him do it. It's God's gift from start to finish! We don't play the major role. If we did, we'd probably go around bragging that we'd done the whole thing! No, we neither make nor save ourselves. God does both the making and saving. He creates each of us by Christ Jesus to join him in the work he does, the good work he has gotten ready for us to do, work we had better be doing.
>
> *Ephesians 2:7-10 MSG*

And in response to God's extraordinary gift of salvation...

> So here's what I want you to do, God helping you: Take your everyday, ordinary life—your sleeping, eating, going-to-work, and walking-around life – and place it before God as an offering. Embracing what God does for you is the best thing you can do for him. Don't become so well-adjusted to your culture that you fit into it without even thinking. Instead,

> fix your attention on God. You'll be changed from the inside out. Readily recognize what he wants from you, and quickly respond to it. Unlike the culture around you, always dragging you down to its level of immaturity, God brings the best out of you, develops well-formed maturity in you.
>
> *Romans 12:1-2 MSG*

Jesus isn't interested in teaching you about religion, but about life – how to live your *real life.* And it's essential for disciples to have a plan for carrying out the decision that they've made to devote themselves to becoming like their Master – to increasingly live in the character and grace of Jesus. Serious and devoted apprentices of Jesus Christ systematically and progressively rearrange how they live their lives under the guidance of God's Word and by the power of God's Spirit. Why do we do this? Because we trust Christ and believe that living as he lived is the best way to live our one and only life. When we trust Christ, it means that we want to be with Jesus as much as we possibly can. When we set our minds on Christ, what comes our way is life and peace. If you want to know God's will for your life, this is the starting place: it is for you to be conformed (and transformed) into the image of Christ, changed from the inside out by the work of the Holy Spirit.

We are invited to choose God in all of our normal day-to-day routines. Every moment, we can choose to spend it *with God*.

That's how we "take hold of that life which is life indeed" (2 Timothy 6:19).

We aren't trying to earn God's love or favor – that's not required. Rather, we're learning to live in his everyday grace, reminded that the Gospel isn't a one-time message but a lifetime reality, that the Gospel isn't about earning anything, but simply about receiving all that God has for us. It's the Gospel of grace!

Made for More

3.5 COMMUNITY

After having a meal together, take a few minutes to share with the group: What's one thing that you see God doing in your life right now?

Now, go ahead and read the following paragraphs out loud before discussing the questions that follow.

1. Disciples proactively strive to keep learning to do all the things Jesus said to do (the big things and the small things). And since Jesus is the *good Master* who teaches us about life, we must take our cues from him as we aspire to learn how to live like him. The best way to learn how to do life with God is to discover how to integrate him into ordinary moments of life. If you're a student, how can you study or attend class like Jesus would? If you work in retail or customer service, what will your response be when you run into problems and difficulties with people? Does it look like the response Jesus might have? No matter what a typical day looks like, true apprentices of Jesus think deeply about how they are going to live their everyday lives in the same way that Jesus would if he was in their place.

Discuss: What's one thing you could change in your approach to your work, your schooling, or how you interact with your family? In other words, how can you set your mind on Christ as you engage in these activities?

2. Here's one way that the Apostle Paul describes how to integrate our faith into our everyday lives:

> **Whatever you do, whether in word or deed,** *do it all in the name of the Lord Jesus.*
>
> *Colossians 3:17*

To live "in the name of the Lord Jesus" involves living in alignment with the godly character and kingdom values of Jesus.

Imagine that your life started to look increasingly more like what Jesus' character and values would look like if he were living in your place. That means that we maintain integrity, embody humility, extend compassion, speak truth, take initiative to face and resolve relational conflict, proactively serve others, and consistently walk closely with God. But before you get too overwhelmed, be reminded that God doesn't require you to live this way on your own – it is only by God's Spirit who empowers you. It is by grace that we live this way. Yes, some human effort is required, however your focus must remain on drawing your strength from God in the context of a relationship with him. You are a learner, a work in progress. You are discovering how to set your mind and fix your eyes on Jesus every day and in every way. As you remain connected to Christ in an interactive, daily, personal relationship, you get empowered and equipped by the Holy Spirit to be conformed to the very character and life of Jesus Christ. Over time, when you spend time with Jesus, you will naturally (or shall I say, *supernaturally*) begin to resemble him – in how you react when you're offended or hurt, in how you behave in certain scenarios, and in how you talk to others who don't speak well of you.

Let's reflect on what an ordinary day in your life could look like as you seek to emulate Christ.

Consider the possibility of inviting Jesus to spend one ordinary day with you. If you can learn how to live one day with Jesus, with your mind set on him and your eyes fixed on him, then you can learn how to live your entire life with him in that way. And the measure that you discover how to do this will be the measure of transformation that you experience!

Discuss: On a typical day, how often are you aware of God's presence or God's activity in your day-to-day life? We encourage you to be transparent, honest, and vulnerable. This question isn't intended to make you feel bad, rather, it's to help elevate your awareness about God's presence in your life. You won't grow or change if you don't see and acknowledge where you are – so go ahead and keep it real on this question.

Discuss: What daily habits could you adjust in your life to help you increase your awareness of God's presence and experience his everyday grace in your life?

For example, when I get dressed each morning, it's my prompt to pray through the armor of God (Ephesians 6:10-20). When I drive to work, my daily practice is to play worship music and invite God to be the leader of my life. When I open my laptop each day, I pray a short prayer that my work would honor and glorify God. I express gratitude for providing a job, giving me motivation to work, and for the opportunities that come because of my work. When I have an appointment with someone, I try to always remember to pray for that person before and/or after our time together (or sometimes I pray with them or ask them if they need prayer). This is not my way of bragging, far from it. Truth is, I need prompts to remind me to connect with God (because I forget). Simply put, these are concrete examples from my life that help me remain aware of God's presence. They help remind me that God is at work in my ordinary life and in the lives of others all around me.

Are there specific ways that you could rearrange and reprioritize any aspects of your life so that you can see the reality and presence of God more consistently? Go ahead and jot down a few ideas that come to mind. Be prepared to share with the group.

Pray for each other to close out the night.

3.6 FOCUS

Jesus' invitation to be his apprentice is an extraordinary opportunity for us as human beings. He offers us access to a personal relationship with our Creator. And if we open the door of our hearts and receive his invitation, everything in our lives will change. But that doesn't mean that we are doing the changing in our own effort. Instead, God is the one who does the changing, or shall we say, the transforming.

Discovering the Abundant Life

As we begin to walk with God, we will learn what it means to experience his abounding grace. We will begin to feel and know the power of the Holy Spirit. As disciples, God desires that we experience his grace *in abundance* every single day. Truth is, we're often not looking for it. Or perhaps we don't slow down long enough to see it or experience it. Or maybe we simply don't live in the present in a way that invites God's Spirit and grace into our daily life.

When Jesus Christ offers "life to the fullest" to every one of his disciples, he is offering us an opportunity of a lifetime. He invites us to walk with him in a way that we will experience this "abundant life," and he knows that when we do, it'll be the best life we could ever have. This way of living comes to us *by grace*, and it's up to us to walk in this way of life.

Here are a few different translations of John 10:10 that articulate the words that Jesus wants us to hear, know, and fully experience.

I came that they may have life and have it abundantly. (ESV)

My purpose is to give them a rich and satisfying life. (NLT)

My purpose is to give life in all its fullness. (LB)

I came that they may have *and* enjoy life, and have it in abundance [to the full, till it overflows]. (AMP)

Guess what? It gets even better. Jesus doesn't just offer us Life.

He *is* **Life.**

Jesus once said:

> I am the bread of life. If you come to My table and eat, you will never go hungry. Believe in Me, and you will never go thirsty.
>
> *John 6:35*

On another occasion, he said:

> I am the resurrection and the source of all life; those who believe in me will live even in death.
>
> *John 11:25*

And yet, in another moment, he declared:

> **I am the way, the truth, and the life! Nobody comes to the Father except through me.**
>
> *John 14:6*

Self-Reflection

What do you long for right now? Really ponder that question.

Now, bring your longings to God and surrender your life and your desires to him. Ask him to speak to you about your longings. Also, be reminded that Jesus can satisfy your deepest soul longings like no one or nothing else can. He is Life. He is the source of life. And he offers you life in all its fullness.

3.7 REST

David was a "man after God's heart" (Acts 13:22). We hope the following prayer from David's life will stir your spirit to pray like he did.

> Your steadfast love is better than life itself, so my lips will give You *all my* praise.
>
> *Psalm 63:3*

Take a few minutes to give God praise for who he is and what he's done for you. Rest in his unconditional and tender love for you as well as his promise of life – both abundant life and eternal life. Meditate on his love for you. Allow his life and peace to rest upon you.

> "What comes into our minds when we think about God is the most important thing about us." – A.W. Tozer

WEEK 4

AN UNEXPECTED CALLING

Follow my example as I follow the example of Christ.
1 Corinthians 11:1

4.1 PREPARATION

When my son was ten, he expressed some meaningful gratitude to his mom with some simple, yet profound words.

"Mom, you're so good at teaching me about life."

He was not only sweet and affirming to his mom, he was expressing sincere gratitude. With his words, he provided a snapshot of a longing that all of us have from our early years: We long to know *how to live life.*

When Jesus comes along and invites us to follow him, he's not inviting us to be part of a religion, nor is he simply asking us to ascribe to a set of Christian beliefs. Instead, **Jesus invites us to discover** *how to live life – according to God's divine design.* Then, once we endeavor on that journey of following Jesus, everything about how we live begins to change.

Although the path we choose in life can end up taking any number of directions, we've all learned how to live life from somebody (or a group of somebodies). That's true for me, you, and every human being.

Let's ponder that for a moment.

Who taught YOU about life?

To say it another way: *whose disciple are you?*

At the beginning of our life story, most of us are disciples of our parent(s) who we grew up with. They taught us about life. For some, that journey was a very good thing. Life provided you with people who helped produce a strong and good foundation for who you are today. For others, that journey wasn't so positive. Maybe your life included varying degrees of bad circumstances from heartbreak, abuse, loss, or tragedy. We acknowledge that to go down this path of introspection could be painful and difficult. But for now, our main point is that whatever road you've traveled, from a young age we all learned how to live from someone. And thankfully, this process is ongoing and self-correcting.

As we move through adolescence and toward young adulthood, we become disciples of a small number of other people. This may include grandparents, teachers, coaches, friends, mentors, or other significant individuals who have been present or instrumental in our lives. This small circle of crucial women and men has impacted how we live our lives today – for better or worse. Some of them provided guidance in moments of major decisions. Perhaps some helped us know how to respond to tragedy or loss. Others might have shaped the development of our spirituality and beliefs, character and identity, relational perspective and self-image, psychological integration and worldview, and/or our life priorities and values. Most of us don't fully realize how much these people have affected who we are and how we live today.

Throughout the New Testament, we find this same reality. The Apostle Paul was one of the most instrumental spiritual leaders in human history. He was discipled by Barnabas. He was also trained and educated by Gamaliel, a disciple maker. Paul discipled Titus, Lydia, and Philemon. He also discipled Timothy, who discipled Eunice and many others in the church at Ephesus.

When we step back and look at the broader scope of Scripture, we find Abigail being discipled by David, Joshua by Moses,

Aquila and Priscilla by the great theologian and teacher Apollos. Mordecai was guided by his young niece, Esther. Naomi discipled young Ruth. Elijah was a spiritual guide for Elisha. Deborah was a disciple maker of Barak. Elizabeth invested profoundly in Mary's life (the mother of Jesus). Examples of how people shaped the lives of others through relationships like these go on and on throughout the Scriptures. These people didn't take this task for granted, rather they intentionally chose to pass on to others what they knew to be true about life. They invested in people with purpose.

While it is true that we become apprentices of Jesus, we also become apprentices of other people. And these people impact who we become. Intentional and purposeful relationships have always been part of God's economy. Relationships are a critical aspect of life and formation for every modern-day disciple. Just as God used a community of people to shape the women and men throughout the Scriptures, he will use others to teach us how to live our lives. We are all disciples of the many people who have influenced us. We learned about life from them. We became who we are today as a result of being molded by them. Some of them were intentional, and others were not. But either way, they had an impact on who we are today.

As we move forward in our lives, we must also recognize that our lives will impact others in ways that we won't and don't fully realize. If we want to truly have a lasting impact, we must learn to build purposeful relationships. We must choose to invest in others with intentionality. As disciples, not only do we learn how to live from others – people learn how to live from us.

In essence, we were designed by God to be disciples *and* disciple makers.

We were created to learn from others how to live. And, we were created to teach and guide others how they are to live.

We are called to BE disciples and to MAKE disciples.

STUDY

A few years ago, curiosity led me to read through all four gospels (Matthew, Mark, Luke, and John), with one primary thing in mind:

With whom did Jesus spend most of his time?

What I discovered had a deep and lasting impact on my way of living. In virtually every chapter, Jesus was **with his disciples**. Whether he was performing a miracle, healing a sick person, or preaching to a large crowd, his disciples were always **with him.**

As I read through these four biographical accounts of Jesus, his intentionality in relationship-building captured my attention. Although teaching, preaching, and doing other supernatural works were all central to his ministry, the relational proximity and focused intentionality that he maintained with his disciples stood out most. Without question, building strong relationships with his disciples was central to him accomplishing his purpose.

For Jesus, fostering purposeful relationships was the context for fulfilling God's mission and doing the Father's will.

This was how he lived. It's also how he taught his apprentices to live: with intentionality and purpose in their relationships and their mission. If we are going to be disciples who make disciples, relational proximity and focused intentionality are essential.

Notice how one gospel writer connects Jesus' relational proximity to his missional focus.

> Jesus appointed twelve, that they might *be with him* and who he could *send out to spread the good news...*
> Mark 3:14

From the beginning of his ministry, and at every turn on his way to fulfilling his Father's will, Jesus built intentional relationships with people whom he believed had the potential to be changed and bring change. He taught and modeled how to live in the reality of what he called *the kingdom of God*. He invited individuals to walk with him so that he could show them how to live a new way – *God's way*. Jesus knew that the only way for human beings to discover what it means to live in the kingdom of God was for them to observe his life and his mission up close and personal. He also knew that his time on earth was limited, so he wanted to find people to whom he could entrust his heart, vision, and mission.

Throughout the gospels, we constantly find Jesus inviting his disciples to not only spend time with him, but to continue to learn how to live out his mission from him (i.e. to make disciples who make disciples).

I love how *The Message* translation puts it:

> Walk with me and work with me – watch how I do it. Learn the unforced rhythms of grace.
> Matthew 11:29

As Jesus walked among us, he knew that relational proximity would foster lasting impact. He also realized that he needed to model a relationship-focused way of disciple making so that after he had departed, his followers would know how to reproduce what they were experiencing with him. Jesus' way of disciple making was always relational, mostly informal, and remarkably intentional. The evidence of his impact was seen in the whole-life transformation of his disciples. Not only were they discovering what the kingdom of God was all about, they were learning to live in a new way. Over time, everything they thought they knew about life started to get turned upside down.

God has brought many mentors into my life over the years who have impacted me in various ways. One man who graciously chose to invest in my life was Erwin. Quite often, he would invite a group of guys to his house to play basketball. We had tons of fun together playing game after game of competitive backyard basketball. But as you'd expect, trash talking and disputing foul calls weren't absent from our times together . Yet, despite all the fun times we had, the most impactful part wasn't the basketball. It was the conversations that happened off the court. As we sweat profusely and competed intensely, meaningful conversations would emerge – and people's lives were being impacted in so many ways. Why? Because in that backyard, things may have appeared casual and informal, but there was more going on. People were always invited with intentionality. They were the people Erwin wanted to invest in relationally. Sometimes that was a staff member. Other times, it was a non-believer or neighbor. But there was purpose with the invitation as well as the conversations that ensued.

I still remember many moments that inspired me to live differently. For example, more than once, I watched my mentor and pastor share the Gospel with someone who was playing basketball. In a few cases, I looked on as he led someone in a prayer to receive Christ as their Savior right there in the backyard. I got a front row seat to see his passion, boldness, and willingness to share his faith when the opportunity presented itself. I also remember moments when Erwin offered insight into my personal life, guidance for my leadership, and encouragement in my calling and gifting. Again, this all looked informal, but Erwin was extremely intentional. As a result, much disciple making happened on the backyard blacktop – often when people didn't even realize it was happening.

This perspective and approach are also what we observe in the gospels, as we watch Jesus Christ travel through ordinary moments in his life with others. Along the way, he teaches, guides, challenges, instructs, and shares the Good News. Embedded in the conversations of life are disciple-making moments – lots of them! And as we see many of these people's lives unfold, we also get to observe the transformational work of God.

4.3 CHANGE

In the early church narrative, we see Paul's life being put on display as an example for others to follow.

> ...some of the people *became followers of Paul* and believed. Among them was Dionysius, a member of the Areopagus, also a woman named Damaris, and a number of others.
>
> *Acts 17:34*

Notice that Dionysius and Damaris – and numbers of others – became *followers of Paul* on their way to becoming followers of Christ.

Wait, aren't we talking about following Jesus, not following Paul?

Yes. And no.

We know that Paul wasn't a cult leader, false prophet, or heretic who was trying to lead people astray. Instead, with a careful reading of the Scriptures, we discover that God's intention all along has been to propel the movement of Jesus followers through intentional relationships. Since people can't follow Jesus in the same way others followed him in the first century, we become the real life, concrete examples of Jesus to other people. That means that on our way to becoming more like Christ, there will be people who follow us first on their way to following Christ.

Maybe your first thought is, "Wait a minute, I am unqualified, imperfect, and flawed. If someone wants to learn how to follow Jesus, looking at my life as an example is not a good idea." If that's what enters your mind, you're just where you need to be.

Just think about the disciples who Jesus invested in and trusted to propel his critical mission. Perhaps the three best-known disciples were Peter, James, and John. We know they didn't always get it right. And there are plenty of examples of that from the gospels. In addition, we know that the disciples Jesus selected were described as "ordinary and unschooled" (Acts 4:13). To the outsider, they were unlikely choices. They were certainly not who others would have deemed the best of the best. Yet, that's whom Jesus chose to pass on his mission – ordinary people like you and me.

Jesus chose young people who messed up more than we even know. And all along, Jesus was confident that with God's help, they would be the ones to jettison the kingdom of God forward. Hopefully, that at least makes you feel a little better about being someone who is called to represent Christ to others and show them how to follow Christ by how you live.

When we dig even deeper into the New Testament, we learn that Paul was keenly aware of his checkered past, as well as his imperfections and flaws. In fact, he frequently mentioned his inadequacies. On one occasion, he told his disciple Timothy that he was the "chief among sinners" (1 Timothy 1:15). But what Paul and those first disciples discovered was:

God uses unqualified, imperfect, and flawed people to be living examples of Christ to others. He looks for those who are broken yet humbly seek to be restored and transformed by God.

One important truth that Paul repeats several times in the New Testament is the phrase, ***follow my example.***

> *Follow my example* as I follow the example of Christ.
> *1 Corinthians 11:1*
>
> You yourselves know how you ought to *follow our example.* We were not idle when we were with you; we did this in order to offer ourselves, our whole lives, as a model for you to imitate.
> *2 Thessalonians 3:7-9*
>
> Join together in *following my example*, brothers and sisters, and just as you have us as a model, keep your eyes on those who live as we do.
> *Philippians 3:17*

When it comes to being a disciple of Jesus, we are to do exactly what Paul and the early disciples did. As we share the Gospel and call people to follow Christ, we stand in the gap and become living examples of Christ-like character to others – as imperfectly as we may do it.

There is a significant weight of responsibility in teaching people how to live like Christ, but isn't that what makes our lives count for something eternal?

The significant responsibility reminds us that we have a high calling that comes with following Jesus. Every disciple has this high calling, and that underscores the fact that Jesus really does believe in you and in who you can become. He wants you to embrace your critical role in teaching, guiding, and training others about how to live life (according to Jesus and his kingdom). That is not just what the people called to ministry do – that is the essence of discipleship for all of us! And if that still feels unsettling or intimidating, join the rest of us who know we'll probably never get it right. It is a sobering reality, but the fact is, God intends that people learn what it means to follow Christ by observing how you follow Christ.

ACTION

In one New Testament letter, Paul writes this to the church at Corinth:

> …you are living letters written by Christ, not with ink but by the Spirit of the living God – not carved onto stone tablets but on the tablets of tender hearts.
>
> *2 Corinthians 3:2*

Paul is underscoring the way that the message of Christ travels: through people, and as a result of the Spirit of God at work in and through his tribe of Jesus followers. In the greater context of this passage, we discover the importance of human beings influencing other human beings. There were people in Paul's life who impacted him. And there were people in Paul's life who he impacted. We are reminded that the impact of the Gospel travels best from person to person through relationships and by the power of God's Spirit. We see the mission of Christ advancing through one purposeful and intentional relationship at a time.

Make no mistake – you are called to live on mission.

Remember when Jesus told his disciples that he's going to train them up to be "fishers of men" (Matthew 4:19)? And remember when he told them to go out into the world and make other disciples? Well, that's Jesus' strategy for the Church to grow, expand, and multiply. This strategy isn't something that Jesus only told church leaders or missionaries to do. He called every follower of Jesus to live on mission with him. That includes you and me, and every disciple.

After three years of following Jesus, Jesus says this to his disciples:

> **As you go throughout the world, make apprentices [disciples] for me from all kinds of people, immersing them in the reality of God, and teaching them to do everything I have commanded you...**
>
> Matthew 28:19-20 (PAR)

Notice the context of relationship building in the disciple-making process. After spending an immense amount of time investing in his disciples (three years), Jesus was ready to send them out. They were equipped and envisioned to advance the mission. They were united around one cause and one purpose. They began to share with the world that there's one ultimate destiny that awaits them – *if they would put their trust in Christ*.

In essence, this is what Jesus had been saying to them all along. It's what crescendos near the end of his life on earth. Basically, this is what he's telling them:

> These past three years have been about showing you how to live differently. I know you don't quite have it perfected, but that's not the requirement. I chose you *just as you are* to go out into the world and live as transformed disciples *and* disciple makers. As you continue learning how to live like Christ and walk in obedience, remember to bring others with you. As you do life, do it with others with intentionality. Be radically inclusive and always invite others to take

their next step in their journey with God. Remember that people are always observing your life – those who follow Jesus, and those who don't. Continue to emulate me and everything that I've taught you, in the grace and power of the Spirit. Along the way, share the gospel with everyone you can. Do it with wisdom, humility, and courage. Represent me well, but also remember the grace and forgiveness that's available to you when you make mistakes.

Be a witness to what I'm doing in your life, and continue to spread this Good News far and wide through every relationship you have.

Never stop communicating the love and grace of God to every person you know. And beyond communicating it to others, make sure you are living it out. This redemptive love is available to every human being on the planet and I have called you to show this love to the world. You were made to live with this divine purpose! And remember this: no matter what, I will always be with you as you participate in carrying out God's grand mission, for his glory!"

The Vision of Jesus

After Jesus leaves the earth, we see how his vision unfolds in the New Testament book of Acts (and later, beyond). When we look at other leaders in the New Testament, we observe a high level of focused intentionality in disciple making. It's clear that early church leaders spread the Good News *through purposeful relationships*. As the Church grew, these leaders walked alongside new converts to help them cultivate their newfound relationship with God and discover a new way of living. In the first century, when people's lives were being changed by the Gospel, women and men sought to reproduce their faith and life in others. As people heard and experienced the Good News, they naturally and instinctively became relational conduits who transmitted the Gospel to others. Multiplication was happening. Not simply through church leaders, but through everyday, ordinary followers of Jesus.

We discover in the New Testament that the Apostle Paul invested in and cared for at least forty-seven women and men in significant fashion. Many of these individuals were people whom he partnered with to plant more than sixteen churches. Part of his core strategy involved identifying people to be on his team as they lived out God's mission together. Whether people were starting small groups of new Jesus followers, making tents as their vocation, or sitting next to each other in jail, Paul's team remained gospel-centered, mission-focused, and relationship-driven. He was always trying to reproduce other disciple makers through relational proximity and focused intentionality.

For Paul, discipleship wasn't something that could be reduced to a classroom setting, nor was it done simply by listening to a sermon or attending a small-group Bible study. Paul's emphasis was relationship-oriented, gospel-focused, and mission-driven. His primary way of discipling others was an integrated way of living his life. He chose to be engaged in the lives of others – believers and unbelievers. He prayed for them, served them, loved them, cared for them, and invested into their lives in hopes that God would use his investment to make an eternal impact. And that's what happened!

Multiplying Disciples

On one occasion, Paul wrote a letter to a faith community in a city called Thessalonica. He had planted this church and cared for these freshly redeemed Jesus followers. We see that he had departed from them during one of his missionary journeys, however, he never forgot about this precious faith community. In 1 Thessalonians 1:6-7, we find some potent words that he shared with those people in Thessalonica when they were going through hard times.

> You became imitators of us and of the Lord, for you welcomed the message in the midst of severe suffering with the joy given by the Holy Spirit. And so you became a model to all the believers in Macedonia and Achaia.

Paul affirmed that they were "imitators" of the Lord Jesus, and of "us" (Paul, Silas, and Timothy). He encouraged this faith community who had welcomed the Gospel message and seen lives transformed as a result. He pointed out that the Thessalonians had become "a model to others in Macedonia and Achaia." They are described as a fellowship of Jesus followers who cared for one another and who spurred each other on in aligning their lives with God's grand mission. These Thessalonians embodied intentional community with one another, viewing their integrated relationships as part of their discipleship journey. They were learning how to live life and teaching others how to live life. Along the way, God sent leaders like Paul to shape their lives, and it's evident that he was also using them to shape the lives of others – despite being brand new Jesus followers, many of whom had just come out of living pagan lifestyles. These are the people we see God using to make an eternal impact!

These disciples understood that for human flourishing to occur, a life-giving and relationally-focused community had to be present – and that's what they were! Through their network of relationships, the Good News was spreading far and wide. Lives were being transformed, beginning with their own. Eternities were being changed because they were passing on what they had received. And heaven was celebrating, while God was being glorified in the lives of these people.

Just as Jesus cultivated disciple multiplication, we see Paul (and others) doing the same. These cultural change agents valued and cultivated intentional community. They understood the importance of relational proximity and connectivity in spreading the Gospel and advancing the kingdom of God. What we see throughout the New Testament clarifies the calling of every modern-day Jesus follower.

The way to cultivate the deepest and greatest kind of impact in our lives is by living with relational proximity and focused intentionality as we carry out the mission of God.

This is our path to discovering our purpose and living a life of significance and impact.

This is the ethos of a discipleship culture.

This is the way of the disciple – and the disciple maker.

Michael's Story

I met Michael at a restaurant. At first, it seemed to be a random coincidence when our two paths crossed. But we clicked right away, and a new friendship began. Michael was an impressive guy. He was a young entrepreneur who ran an athletic training business. He worked with clients from all over the city of Chicago. And since his expertise was in such high demand, the cost to hire him kept rising. What he offered was exceptional, so people continued to come his way. Not only that, but he had a sharp mind and was relationally intelligent – and it just seemed like everything he touched turned to gold. At a young age, he had become successful, wealthy, and let's just say, he appealed to the ladies.

Early in our friendship, Michael seemed incredibly happy and optimistic about life. I mean, what could be better for him? To anyone who knew him, life seemed like it was about as good as it could get. However, as our friendship grew and I got to know him better, I listened more closely to his story, and began to notice that there was more than meets the eye. Underneath the exterior was an undisclosed struggle. I discovered that everything wasn't going quite as well as it seemed. As we built trust, I probed a little deeper. One day, Michael shared with me that he was an alcoholic.

We began to openly talk about his struggles and fears. He told me about his involvement with AA, and that his meetings and sponsor was helping him. As the months passed, we discussed spiritual things. In time, his spiritual search intensified, and he began externalizing his deeper internal questions about who God was and what it meant to relate to him. He had already come to believe in God (cognitively speaking), but there was still a void. At lunch one day, he asked me how to find meaning in life and how he could know if God was real. All our conversations had significant components to them, but what really fueled it all were Michael's fears and struggles. And because he was opening his heart, he was beginning to move closer to the God who created him. The day came when he was finally ready to follow Jesus.

One week after Michael became a follower of Christ, he asked me if I could help him start a small group with his friends from AA. I told him, "Sure, let's do it!" We decided to start the group the following week. All week, Michael invited some of his friends until the night arrived. I had helped Michael prepare for the night, guiding him in how to lead a group study until he felt prepared. Neither of us knew who would show up, if anyone, but we were ready to go, prayerful, and excited.

To our delight, twelve of his friends from AA showed up to the Bible study that night, none of whom were followers of Jesus. We were shocked, especially learning that most of them were indifferent or resistant to Christianity.

After some small talk, we circled up in the living room. I was ready to watch Michael lead the group, but was also feeling anxious about how the night would go. After Michael called everyone together and welcomed them, he looked at me and said, "Alright Steve, you can start the Bible study." I was caught off guard, and my heart was pumping fast. All I knew to do was to start with a question.

The first thing that popped into my mind was, **"Does anyone see God working in their life?"**

In truth, I was just trying to buy some time to regroup and get my mind around how to facilitate the night. But the responses to my question ended up going on for a while. Michael's friends began to pour out their hearts. They openly shared real fears, intense struggles, and honest doubts about God. Considering that I had led a countless number of small groups and Bible studies over the years, I was rather amazed to watch it all unfold.

At one point, I opened the Bible, read a passage about Jesus, and simply asked them what they thought about the text. Again,

I listened as they shared with authenticity and vulnerability. There were tears at certain points, and even a moment when I prayed for a couple of them who were going through some very difficult things. It was amazing to watch things unfold, all because Michael took some risks to invite a few friends into a deeper dialogue about God.

You may be interested to know that the group continued for many weeks. Along the way, Michael shared his own story, including his journey to find God and follow God. During those weeks, several others in the group expressed how Michael was changing, that he was a different person now. I saw it too. What was happening? His life was being transformed by God. No, he wasn't living a "perfect life" – whatever that might mean. But he was changing, growing, and living differently. Over the course of a few months, Michael started to ask his friends what they thought about Jesus, and whether they were interested in following him. Several of them eventually said yes to Jesus, which was incredible to see. It was all quite an amazing adventure.

Michael is a living example of a person not only being a disciple of Jesus, but being willing to put his imperfect life on display so that his friends might just experience Jesus as well. He came alongside some friends that he really cared about and in essence said, "Follow me as I learn what it means to follow Christ." What ensued was just that. Some of them followed Michael's life and leadership and watched him change before their very eyes – and then they found themselves ready to make a change as well. Michael became a disciple, and quickly became a disciple maker. Like Paul, he invited others to follow him as he followed Jesus. Michael was far from who he wanted to become as a Christ follower, but he opened up his life and watched as God used him to make an impact on those who also needed to find God!

4.5 COMMUNITY

If you want to make progress as a disciple of Jesus, you must remember that life change happens primarily in the context of community. The reality is: you either grow and thrive *together* or you won't end up growing much at all.

It's important to think specifically about the people who have shaped your life and helped you grow.

Who has discipled you?

It's also important to think about the impact your life has had on others.

Who have you helped grow? Who have you discipled?

After sharing a meal together during your community time, take a few moments to read this question and these two short passages of Scripture. It will inform and guide your discussion time in just a few moments.

What observations and insights do you notice in the following passages when it comes to living with purpose and intentionality in your relationships?

> Discover creative ways to encourage others and to motivate them toward acts of compassion, doing beautiful works as expressions of love. This is not the time to pull away and neglect meeting together,

as some have formed the habit of doing, because we need each other! In fact, we should come together even more frequently, eager to encourage and urge each other onward as we anticipate that day dawning.

Hebrews 10:24-25 MSG

You are always and dearly loved by God! So robe yourself *with virtues of God*, since you have been divinely chosen to be holy. Be merciful as you endeavor to understand others, and be compassionate, showing kindness toward all. Be gentle and humble, unoffendable in your patience with others. Tolerate the weaknesses of those in the family of faith, forgiving one another in the same way you have been graciously forgiven by Jesus Christ. If you find fault with someone, release this same gift of forgiveness to them. For love is supreme and must flow through each of these virtues. Love becomes the mark of true maturity.

Colossians 3:12-14 MSG

Sharing: Invite each person in the group to share about one person in their life who has poured into them. In other words, who has discipled them or helped them grow? And then describe what that looked like in real life?

After everyone has shared, transition the discussion to sharing about one person that they are currently discipling or have had the opportunity to encourage or affirm lately. How is disciple making going right now? What is going well? What is challenging? For those who aren't discipling anyone, rest easy.

Perhaps you can share what is challenging to overcome when you consider trying to invest in someone else.

> NOTE: Make sure everyone in the group takes time to listen to each person, maintaining a posture of listening and learning. Pay attention to discipleship principles and practices that everyone can learn from. Then, invite everyone to think about personal applications in response to the discussions.

What are the challenges in living out and applying what you've been hearing in your everyday lives as disciples and disciple makers? Identify one action step that you can take to apply what you've been learning this week. Is there anything that God has been stirring in your heart as the discussions have progressed? Is there anything about your perspective, approach, or priorities that needs some adjustment?

To wrap up your time, take a few minutes to pray in your group as a response to what God is stirring up in you.

4.6 FOCUS

Paul lived with a remarkable passion to make disciples. It wasn't primarily about preaching the Gospel from a platform to a larger group of people, though that was one important aspect of his specific calling. But notice that he was primarily focused on sharing his life with people as he sought to embody the mission of God. He understood the importance of people being able to "watch his life" as he lived as a disciple and disciple maker. He was a living example of someone who had been – and was continuing to be – transformed by God.

In one letter to the Thessalonians, Paul said:

> "...so we cared for you. Because we loved you so much, we were delighted to share with you not only the gospel of God, but our lives as well."
>
> *1 Thessalonians 2:8*

Over many years, an uncountable number of people were inspired, encouraged, and challenged by his unwavering allegiance and full devotion to his Savior. In his everyday relationships, Paul intentionally communicated the truths, values, and principles of following Jesus. He lived out biblical values in community, invested in others, and cared for people along the way. He also invited people on the same path that he was on. Along the way, he reproduced like-minded individuals, as well as communities of people who were seeking God and inviting others into the same quest for transformation into Christlikeness.

> You have heard me teach things that have been confirmed by many reliable witnesses. Now teach these truths to other trustworthy people who will be able to pass them on to others.
>
> 2 Timothy 2:2 NLT

Reality Check: What kind of life are you inviting people to imitate?

The Scriptures never tell us to be a perfect example, but they do call us to be the "salt of the earth" and the "light of the world" (Matthew 5:13-14). That means you have the capacity to influence. It also means that other people should be able to tell the difference between a follower of Jesus and someone who doesn't yet follow him. The reality is: there are probably some aspects of your life that have started to look more like Christ, and there are other aspects of your life that need some improvement and adjustments.

There are many components to your life to think about, but as a way of bringing focus, let's start by putting a spotlight on a few areas of your life where God's transforming power still needs to do its work so that your light can shine brighter. After all, when the Gospel truly transforms your life, the evidence is seen in a holistic way, in all aspects of your life. That means that the Gospel can transform your relationships, change how you approach work, finances, conflict, and friendship. When you're transformed by the Gospel, you find purpose and meaning, you find love and joy, and you find a peace that suprasses understanding.

Journaling: Here are a few questions that I have in my own journal. I reflect on them on a regular basis – usually monthly

– as one of my intentional spiritual practices. Why? Because it cultivates necessary self-reflection and healthier self-leadership in my life. Plus, it reminds me of who I am in Christ (my Gospel identity) and ensures that I pay close attention to the work that God still needs to do in me. I don't always respond to or answer all the questions. Sometimes, I focus on just a few. Mostly, I pay attention to what needs the most attention in my life at the time.

1. Have I been getting discouraged or anxious about anything lately?

2. What are my current levels of stress, and how has that been affecting my relationships? Use a scale of one to ten to evaluate your stress levels.

3. Have I been consistently complaining, overly critical, or too negative in my conversations with others?

4. Have I been easily irritable, impatient, or snippy with anyone?

5. How often have I been in a hurry lately or felt rushed?

6. Have I been sharp, cunning, or sarcastic with my words? Have I spoken any unwholesome words to anyone, or spoken in a hurtful or demanding way?

7. Am I angry or resentful towards anyone right now? Do I have any unforgiveness in my spirit that's unresolved?

8. Is there a tension or conflict I need to address? Maybe a situation I handled poorly?

9. How well have I been stewarding my finances? Have I been generous? Sacrificial? Servant hearted toward people? Have I remained open handed and open hearted with God regarding the resources God has given me?

10. Have I been experiencing authentic joy?

11. How well have I been treating people? With kindness and tenderness? With respect for others? Is there any way that I've treated someone unlovingly?

12. Have I been a good question asker and genuine listener? Have I focused on others much?

13. How am I doing with rest, Sabbath, and the overall rhythm of my life? Am I maintaining healthy boundaries and creating margin in my life? What would my family say about that?

14. What has been my overall attitude at work? How about my work ethic? Are my relationships at work strong? Is there anything at work that I can do better so that I honor God more? Am I maintaining my integrity at work in every way possible?

15. How are things going with my spouse (if married) and kids (if any)? Is there anything I need to adjust in my parenting or marriage? How about with other family members? Am I honoring God in those relationships? How about my closest friendships?

Take a few moments to journal your thoughts to help you think deeply about the rhythms, habits, and behaviors in your life. You can use the above questions as prompts to get you going, but also feel free to add your own. Just remember to keep the Gospel front and center. Then, invite God to speak to you, shape you, and mold you.

In an effort to take action after your reflections, take a few minutes to pray. Consider what adjustments are needed to make your life one that others could be inspired to emulate. God doesn't need or expect you to be perfect. But, he does call you to live differently as you redefine, refine, and realign your life.

4.7 REST

One Father's Day, my son gave me a canvas to hang on the wall. I put it in my living room to remind me of my own journey of becoming. The canvas says:

> A Son's Prayer: "Dear God, make me the kind of man my daddy is."

> A Father's Prayer: "Dear God, make me the kind of man my son thinks I am."

This reminds me of my own longing to live an honorable life, and become the man that I not yet am but dream of becoming. As my friend Mark Batterson famously said about what real success really is:

> **SUCCESS** is when **those** who **KNOW YOU BEST** actually **RESPECT YOU MOST**.

For a few moments, focus on the longing within *YOU*.

God gave you the desire to become someone better than you already are. However, he doesn't want you to live in shame of who you have not yet become.

God longs for you to know that when you live relationally and personally connected to Jesus, in touch with your deep longings, God's Spirit will do a powerful work in you. He will mold you and then use you in ways that go beyond your understanding. You can rest in the privilege and honor of being used by God – as imperfect as you are – to make a difference in the lives of others. This is the way of the disciple, and it is the way of love.

> "He does not call us to do what he did but to be as he was, permeated with love." – Dallas Willard

> As far as God is concerned, there is a sweet, wholesome fragrance in our lives. It is the fragrance of Christ within us, an aroma to both the saved and the unsaved all around us.
>
> *2 Corinthians 2:15*

WEEK 5

AN UNSELFISH HEART

When you demonstrate the same love I have for you by loving one another, everyone will know that you're my true followers.
John 13:35

PREPARATION

Bill Belichick is known by many as the best football coach of all-time. He's also known for always emphasizing one thing to his players to prepare them for each game. He preaches this over and over again: "Do your job." What is he really saying? He is focusing his team because he recognizes that his players can get distracted by many things during a game. He knows how crucial it is to keep them focused on what they can control – "doing their job." This simple phrase reminds the players what is most important. In essence, they need to know their role and execute it to the best of their ability on every play. And if everyone does their job, together they can become a championship-caliber team.

In similar fashion, when Jesus walked among us, he focused his followers on the most important thing. He often explained how essential this thing was. He said that everything else waned in importance to this one thing. He also told his disciples that if they would do their part to live this out, it would propel the movement of Christ like nothing else – and the whole world would be different.

So, what was the one thing?

At the end of his ministry, Jesus was at his last Passover with his twelve disciples. He had a few final things to share with these guys, but he focused them on *one critical thing*.

> My dear friends, I only have a brief time left to be with you. And then you will search and long for me. But I tell you what I told the Jewish leaders: you'll not be able to come where I am.
>
> John 13:33

Imagine Peter sitting there, perking up and saying, "Wait a minute. You're leaving us? Where exactly are you going? And if you go, I want to go."

Jesus often saw Peter speaking up, so this moment wouldn't surprise Jesus.

The conversation continues, as Jesus brings the one thing into focus.

> I give you now a new commandment: Love each other just as much as I have loved you.
>
> John 13:34a

At first glance, what Jesus said wasn't all that earth shattering. Maybe those disciples even thought they had read things like that in the Old Testament. Maybe they were hoping to hear something more insightful. And perhaps the disciples thought, "Alright Jesus. We got it. Can you keep going please?"

Jesus does elaborate.

> As I have loved you, so you must love one another.
>
> *John 13:34b*

In essence, he's telling his disciples that he wants **love** to characterize their relationships with one another.

> For when you demonstrate the same love I have for you by loving one another, everyone will know that you're my true followers.
>
> *John 13:35*

Love is the one thing. And it is a critical component of building a discipleship culture.

5.2 STUDY

One of the New Testament Greek words for love is ***agape***. When this word gets used in the Scriptures (more than 200 times), it refers to a willful, pure, and sacrificial love. It is the love that God has for humanity. It is a love that intentionally desires the highest good of another. And it is a love that gets demonstrated through action.

Jesus took action to set the greatest example of love. He did it on our behalf and for our eternal benefit.

> For even the Son of Man came not to be served but to serve, and to give his life as a ransom for many.
>
> *Mark 10:45*
>
> Be full of love for others, following the example of Christ who loved you and gave Himself to God as a sacrifice to take away your sins.
>
> *Ephesians 5:2*
>
> Christ loved the church and gave his life for it.
>
> *Ephesians 5:25*

The Scriptures tell us that God is love and that God sent his one and only Son Jesus Christ to die on the cross on our behalf to atone for our sins. This is the essence of the Gospel.

Jesus Christ laid down his life as the ultimate sacrifice to show humanity the full extent of his love.

In grateful response to the Gospel, we love God and others as a result of his love for us. In other words, we learn to love only because he first loved us (1 John 4:19). As we discover and experience God's love in our lives, we begin to be conduits of that love to others.

Here's how the Apostle John says it:

My loved ones, let us devote ourselves to loving one another. Love comes straight from God, and everyone who loves is born of God and truly knows God. Anyone who does not love does not know God, because God is love.

> Because of this, the love of God is a reality among us: God sent His only Son into the world so that we could find true life through Him. This is the embodiment of true love: not that we have loved God first, but that He loved us and sent His unique Son on a special mission to become an atoning sacrifice for our sins. So, my loved ones, if God loved us so sacrificially, surely we should love one another.
>
> *1 John 4:7-11*
>
> This is how we know what love is: Jesus Christ laid down his life for us. And we ought to lay down our lives for our brothers and sisters.
>
> *1 John 3:16*

> **Love means living the way God commanded us to live. As you have heard from the beginning, his command is this: Live a life of love.**
>
> *2 John 1:6*

In Mark 12:28-31, we find what many call the Greatest Commandment. We find Jesus telling us to *agapao* God and our neighbors.

> Now a certain religious scholar overheard them debating. When he saw how beautifully Jesus answered all their questions, he posed one of his own, and asked him, "Teacher, which commandment is the greatest of all?"
>
> Jesus answered him, "The most important of all the commandments is this: 'The Lord Yahweh, our God, is one!' You are to love (*agapao*) the Lord Yahweh, your God, with a passionate heart, from the depths of your soul, with your every thought, and with all your strength. This is the great and supreme commandment. And the second is this: 'You must love (*agapao*) your neighbor in the same way you love yourself.' You will never find a greater commandment than these."

The distinguishing characteristic of Jesus' disciples is not how much we pray. It's not how much biblical knowledge we have. It's not how loud we preach or sing on Sunday. Jesus cares more about whether we are loving God and loving one another than anything else. In essence, Jesus calls us to be all about love. This is what the movement of Christ is all about. This kind of love is central to a healthy discipleship culture.

> Let love be your greatest aim.
>
> *1 Corinthians 14:1*

If we want to value what Jesus values, and if we want to continue our quest to become just like Christ, living a life of love must become our greatest aim.

Anyone can be a *Christian*. But when we consider what it really means to be a disciple, what if we all "did our job?" What if our greatest goal was to love others like Christ loves us?

> And if I were to have *the gift* of prophecy with a profound understanding of God's hidden secrets, and if I possessed unending supernatural knowledge, and if I had the greatest gift of faith that could move mountains, but have never learned to love, then I am nothing.
>
> *1 Corinthians 13:2*

5.3 CHANGE

Several years ago, I had a friend who was searching. He wasn't sure what he was searching for, but he knew that something was missing in his life. He had grown up in a home where his mom was a Buddhist and his dad was an atheist. But now as a young adult, he wasn't sure what he believed. Add to that a couple negative religious experiences, and he wasn't sure that anything about God or religion was something he wanted to pursue.

We met in Los Angeles after he arrived for college. I learned early on that he had a nagging sense of emptiness. As a result, he began to ask some of the deeper questions about life. Along the way, he met a few other Christians who all attended the same church – my church. Surprisingly (he told me later), he liked them. His previous experiences of Christians were altogether negative, partly because they would find out that he was gay, and suddenly, the way he was treated would change. He had a few stories of Christians being unkind and uncaring. These situations were marked by those folks being rude, self-righteous, hypocritical, and judgmental. Needless to say, he didn't like them, nor was he interested in their church or their God.

After getting to know some Christians whom he liked, it was unsettling at first. Thankfully though, he quickly realized that these people were very different. After a few months spent getting to know these new friends, he'd hear them talk about their church and their faith positively. He listened and observed. Then, he made a bold move one day and decided to go to church. He was adamant in letting it be known that he wasn't interested in becoming a Christian, and that he was simply going out of curiosity and perhaps to meet some new friends. As the months went on, he continued to attend, listening intently to the teachings from the Bible. He eventually started attending a small group and experienced a place of belonging.

His story is unique. I still remember when he told me early on what he seemed to tell everyone at our church: "I am not a Christian and never will become one." One day, we were walking together on the sidewalk, and I decided to ask him why he kept attending our church (I assured him that we wanted him to and welcomed him, but that I was curious to know). It was a Christian church with Christian teaching, and most of the people were Christians.

He proceeded to tell me that our church was very different than he expected – and that the people were very different too. They were unlike any religious people he had ever met. That intrigued him. So I probed a little more, continuing to ask a few questions to hear more of his story. I wanted to get to know the deeper questions and curiosities he had.

When I asked him, "What really keeps you coming back? Because you don't really believe what we believe, think how we think, or live how we live."

Suddenly, he grabbed my arm, and stopped me in the middle of the sidewalk in downtown Los Angeles. He looked at me with sincerity and said something I'll never forget.

"The reason I continue to come to your church is because the people at this church love me really well."

That sent chills throughout my body. It impacted me deeply. Love is what compelled his heart… and it was changing him and his perspective about God and his followers. Truth is, people aren't usually turned off by God. They are turned off by his followers.

My friend went on to elaborate. He told me that people respected him for who he was, for being honest about where he was at, and even for owning his own beliefs. He shared how he expected people to force their beliefs on him, and be relentless in trying to convert him. But instead, he said the people shared their faith and the overall Christian message with him, but did it with such grace and gentleness; with kindness and respect. They listened to his story rather than just trying to proclaim their own. They cared about him in so many ways and included him in everything that was happening at the church. All of those things together communicated love. A profound love that impacted his life deeply.

God desires for people to be drawn to the love they see exuding from your life.

What if love became the reputation of the church? What if people who were not followers of Jesus were inspired when they looked at how we treated one another as well as those on the outside? What if an increasing number of people said about our churches, "Wow, the people at this church love others really well." Imagine if people on the outside saw Jesus followers being irrationally generous to each other. Imagine if they saw Christian men honoring women. Imagine if they saw leaders in the church who served others rather than using their power over others. What if they saw Jesus followers treat the "least of these" with dignity and saw them care for the forgotten or unwanted of society? Imagine if they saw us respond to ridicule, persecution, and hatred with tender and tough love. And what if they saw strong and healthy marriages, families who loved one another well, and churches who were radically inclusive?

Jesus longs for us to build communities like that. And he assures us that the kingdom of God will expand when we embody this kind of love. People on the outside will be drawn in because wherever true agape love exists, lives will be impacted and eternities will be altered.

What if employers had such positive experiences with Christ followers that they were always looking to hire one? What if husbands treated their wives with selfless love and utter respect? What if people everywhere wanted to work for a Christ follower because they knew they would be treated well?

If we loved people the way Jesus envisioned us to love people, our impact would be extraordinary – in our local communities, our workplaces, our schools, our cities, our nation, and even our churches. And guess what? According to Scripture, this is the most important thing we can do: to love one another just as Christ loved us. This is "our job." And by God's grace, we have the opportunity and the capacity to love like this, with God's help.

As disciples of Jesus, we are responsible to build communities of people who are characterized by this kind of love. It won't be easy and might get messy, but it is what we must exemplify.

Jesus came on the scene to show us this way of living. And he told us that it would be the thing that God uses to expand our impact in the world.

How do others know if we are disciples of Jesus?

Jesus answers that.

> ...by the way we love one another.

What if we just got this one thing right?

What if people said, "I don't know if I want to be a Christian, but I would like to work for one. I would like to hire one. I want my daughter or son to marry one. Why? Because every Christian I know loves other people really well."

When we get this one thing right (and not until then), the world will know we are disciples by our love. What will follow? People will be drawn to Christ. People's lives will be changed. God will be glorified.

5.4 ACTION

The love that we find Jesus calling out of his followers is not only a sincere love, but an action-oriented love. When this kind of love is embodied, it is evidence of spiritual maturity. Disciples are virtuous people who serve others in love, who live out love in action, and who embody a spiritual maturity that inspires others around them. They love people sincerely. Disciples love people not only with their words but by their actions. They serve people, and are willing to sacrifice at times too. They don't simply talk about love, they live out love in action.

> My children, our love should not be just words and talk; it must be true love, which shows itself in action.
>
> *1 John 3:18*

> For love is supreme and must flow through each of these virtues. Love becomes the mark of true maturity.
>
> *Colossians 3:14*

Let's get more practical by describing how to put love into action. How do we go about loving others like Jesus loved us?

1. Love others is by being genuinely interested in them.

> Give more honor to others than to yourselves. Do not be interested only in your own life, but be interested in the lives of others.
>
> *Philippians 2:3-4*

In this text, we find the Greek word, *skopos*. It means, "to look out for." This is the same term from which we get our words microscope and telescope. Paul tells us to look out for others, to look out for one another's interests, not just our own. He challenges us to pay close attention to other people's lives, to honor them, and to focus on their interests. The first act of loving another human being is always the giving of attention.

Agape love is so intently focused on the other that it forgets itself for a moment. When we are truly loving another person, we lose sight of ourselves and genuinely focus on the other.

When we give someone our focused attention, we're saying to another human being, "I value you enough to give you my most precious assets – my time, my attention, and my presence. I will slow down long enough to listen to you, care for you, seek to understand you, hear your heart, value what you have to say, and accept you where you are. I will truly be present with you, unhurried and unrushed."

> Don't just pretend that you love others: really love them. Be devoted to one another in love. Honor one another above yourselves.
>
> *Romans 12:9-10*

2. Love others by genuinely listening to them.

There's a powerful connection between listening and loving. Here's how David Augsburger makes that connection:

> Being heard is so close to being loved that for the average person, they are almost indistinguishable.

Human beings want to be heard, seen, and known. We don't want to live as anonymous. No one wants to feel invisible. We were designed to live relationally connected to one another so that we can be seen, known, and heard. And if we fail to listen to each other, we'll never know each other the way God designed us to.

We've all interacted with someone who doesn't listen. Perhaps when they talk to us, they want us to listen to them, but as soon as we start to talk, it's like they are on their own track, not seeming to care about anything we're saying. It can be irritating, can't it?

Truth is, we can't control whether someone else listens to us, but we are responsible for whether we choose to listen to others. And to the measure that we do, will be the measure of our love for others.

If you want to love people well, start by taking time to genuinely listen to others. If you want to make a difference in someone's life, listening is a good place to start.

> **Be quick to listen, and slow to speak.**
> *James 1:19*

If we don't take time to truly hear people and genuinely seek to understand them, we will never extend the fullest kind of love to them.

As disciples, we all need to set out to cultivate a listening kind of love. It is a love that we can give to others with the help and empowerment of God. It is a kind of love that human beings need if they are going to feel known.

Most of the time, we underestimate the impact that listening can have on another person. When we listen with sincerity, we are expressing a selfless love towards others. We are establishing a relational and emotional connection. We are cultivating a healthy relational bond. Sincere listening is not only a powerful way to express and extend love for others, it is a consistent trait of Jesus Christ, one he models for us.

When we listen well, people feel seen, heard, and known. And even further, when outsiders experience this kind of listening love, the Gospel spreads. The movement of Jesus is on the verge of being ignited because people will be drawn to Christ because they are drawn to love. Make no mistake, lives will be forever changed when people feel the most loved. And love emerges when we truly listen.

3. Loving other people involves asking intentional, thoughtful questions.

Asking questions goes hand in hand with being genuinely interested in others and listening to them with sincerity. Asking questions helps us take our eyes off ourselves and show someone that we care. We are communicating to another person that their life and unfolding story really matters – to you, and to God. I have an old friend who went to Calcutta years ago and actually got to spend time with Mother Theresa. One thing he said about her was this: "When you were talking with her, you felt like no one in the whole world was more important than you. She would ask sincere questions about your life and then listen to you so intently, like nothing else mattered more than what you were sharing."

Did you ever pay attention to how many questions Jesus asks in the gospels?

> In Matthew, he asks eighty-seven questions.
>
> In Mark, he asks more than sixty questions.
>
> In Luke, he asks 129 questions.
>
> Then, in all four gospels, how do you think he responds to the 183 questions that he gets asked?
>
> Jesus responds with 307 more questions.

That's a lot of questions – especially for a guy who has a lot to say, someone who has a rather important mission to carry out, and a man who already knows EVERYTHING. If anyone had important things to say, truths to proclaim, and sins to rebuke, it was the Son of God. It's remarkable to see how often Jesus slowed down and took time to ask an intentional, thoughtful question. And I imagine that the person he was interacting with felt like no one in the world was more important, or felt more loved, than them.

There were many reasons why Jesus asked questions. There's no doubt that he used questions during his three years in ministry with purpose and intention. By asking questions, he communicated that he cared about people, their life story, and the decisions they were making.

Jesus undoubtedly asked questions because he wanted people to know that they mattered to God and that they were worthy of love.

Sometimes Jesus used questions with religious people while a non-religious person was present. We often see him confronting religious people through questions and extending compassionate love to the non-religious people (see John 8).

It's so easy to forget what a gift it is for people to be asked a thoughtful, caring question. And when we remain present to genuinely listen to their answer, we are living out love in action. When we slow down enough to ask intentional questions, and when we genuinely listen to another person, we communicate that we care about them, that we want to know their story and hear about their life.

If you want to become more like Jesus then you must pursue becoming more interested in people. You must learn to ask people thoughtful and intentional questions followed by sincerely listening to the story of their life. Then, as you listen, pay attention to their needs, their hurts, their worries, and their joys.

Let's be honest: our human tendency is to focus our attention on ourselves. Yet, when we learn how to focus on others with genuine interest in who they are and what's going on in their lives, we express a unique and rare kind of love towards them. You cannot become truly selfless in your living unless you learn to listen well. This way of loving others is Christ-like in character, and it reveals that we have an unselfish heart being formed inside of us.

We may never know the impact of one loving word, one caring conversation, or one listening ear.

Live in true devotion to one another, loving each other as sisters and brothers. Be first to honor others by putting others first.

Romans 12:10

Have sincere love for each other, love one another deeply from the heart.

1 Peter 1:22

Above all, love each other deeply…

1 Peter 4:8

5.5 COMMUNITY

Go ahead and share a meal together to begin the night.

Before getting into the discussion, allow everyone to take a few minutes to assess their own listening skills through a short self-assessment. The only requirement is honesty. You can view this exercise as a step in the growth process for your discipleship journey. And I'm pretty sure that all of us need to improve our listening skills at some level, so we're all in this together.

Circle all statements that you can affirm fully.
(Thanks to Peter Scazzero for inspiration to create a listening assessment)

1. I make a great effort to enter other people's experiences in life.

2. I never catch myself waiting for another person to finish speaking so I can talk.

3. I do not presume to know what the other person is trying to communicate.

4. My close friends would say I listen more than I speak.

5. I do not assume that I understand what the other person means before asking them a follow-up question.

6. When people are angry with me, I am able to listen to their side without getting upset.

7. People share freely with me because they know I listen well.

8. I listen not only to what people say but also for their nonverbal cues, body language, tone of voice, and the like.

9. I give people my undivided attention when they are talking to me.

10. I am able to reflect back and validate another person's feelings with empathy.

11. I am aware of my primary defensive mechanisms when I am under stress, such as placating, blaming, problem solving prematurely, or becoming distracted.

12. I am aware of how the family in which I was raised has influenced my present listening style.

13. In conversations, I don't assume I know what the other person needs to hear.

14. I ask for clarification when I am not clear on something another person is saying rather than attempt to fill in the blanks.

15. I never assume something, especially negative, unless it is clearly stated by the person speaking.

16. When someone else is talking to me, I don't think very much about other things while they are talking.

17. I ask questions when listening rather than try to read others' minds or make assumptions.

18. I don't interrupt or listen for openings to get my point across when someone else is speaking.

19. When I am listening to someone, I am aware of my own personal "hot buttons" that cause me to get angry, upset, fearful, or nervous more quickly.

20. I am aware of my mood and how it impacts a conversation.

If you circled seventeen or more, you are an outstanding listener; thirteen to sixteen, you are a -16 very good listener; ten to twelve means you are a semi-good listener; nine or fewer means you likely need to make some significant changes in how you relate to people.

If you want to be really brave, ask your spouse or closest friend to rate you as a listener.

With your group, take turns sharing what stood out to you with the assessment.

After everyone has an opportunity to share, split up into groups of two or three. Practice asking questions as you seek to get to know someone more deeply. One person goes at a time, for an allotted period of time. It could be anywhere from five to ten minutes. You may want to set a timer so everyone stays on the same track. Remember to ask questions that are thoughtful, intentional, and personal. Seek to get to know what someone is going through, or even just to hear their life story. If you want to extend the time for each group, feel free. The goal here is to get a little bit of practice in listening and asking questions.

At the end of your time together, gather as a group one final time. Share any insights or observations that relate to your own growth process in regards to learning how to love other people more sincerely and selflessly. Maybe you simply want to share one way that God was speaking to you, or one next step you're going to take. Then, close in prayer.

5.6 FOCUS

One of the most poignant examples of love is found in the Gospel of John. After reading this passage from *The Message* translation, we invite you to reflect on the question below.

> Just before the Passover Feast, Jesus knew that the time had come to leave this world to go to the Father. Having loved his dear companions, he continued to love them right to the end. It was suppertime. The Devil by now had Judas, son of Simon the Iscariot, firmly in his grip, all set for the betrayal.
>
> Jesus knew that the Father had put him in complete charge of everything, that he came from God and was on his way back to God. So he got up from the supper table, set aside his robe, and put on an apron. Then he poured water into a basin and began to wash the feet of the disciples, drying them with his apron. When he got to Simon Peter, Peter said, "Master, you wash my feet?"
>
> Jesus answered, "You don't understand now what I'm doing, but it will be clear enough to you later."
>
> Peter persisted, "You're not going to wash my feet – ever!"

> Jesus said, "If I don't wash you, you can't be part of what I'm doing."
>
> "Master!" said Peter. "Not only my feet, then. Wash my hands! Wash my head!"
>
> Jesus said, "If you've had a bath in the morning, you only need your feet washed now and you're clean from head to toe. My concern, you understand, is holiness, not hygiene. So now you're clean. But not every one of you." (He knew who was betraying him. That's why he said, "Not every one of you.") After he had finished washing their feet, he took his robe, put it back on, and went back to his place at the table.
>
> Then he said, "Do you understand what I have done to you? You address me as 'Teacher' and 'Master,' and rightly so. That is what I am. So if I, the Master and Teacher, washed your feet, you must now wash each other's feet. I've laid down a pattern for you. What I've done, you do. I'm only pointing out the obvious. A servant is not ranked above his master; an employee doesn't give orders to the employer. If you understand what I'm telling you, act like it – and live a blessed life.
>
> *John 13:1-17*

As disciples of Jesus, this passage reminds us of who we are called to be – servants (of God and of others). God's desire for his disciples is that we would embody a lifestyle of serving others and blessing others. We've been blessed beyond measure, and with a grateful response, we are called to be a blessing to others. We have a God who gave his life as a ransom for the world... to serve humanity selflessly. Now, he calls us to turn our hearts to the world and serve them by the transforming power of the Holy Spirit.

Reflection: What would it look like in your life to serve and bless people in a unique and wholesome way? Would you take a few moments and pray about who God may want you to serve - or about how God may want you to start serving someone in your life?

Disciples of Jesus actively look to extend love and do good in any and every way.

We can serve our families, volunteer in our churches, or give of our time and resources to our surrounding community. We can serve people at work or at home. We can serve our neighbors and our spouses. We can serve people in need locally and globally. There are endless ways that we can serve. The point is this: Jesus demonstrated servanthood to his disciples as a way of life. He often reminded them how important it was for disciples of Jesus to serve others. And yes, it will require something from us. It might even make us feel uncomfortable. But God made us on purpose and with a purpose. And serving others is an essential way that we live out that purpose.

APPLICATION: What can you do this week to cultivate a new habit of serving others?

5.7 REST

Jesus told his disciples that the movement of Christ is fueled by love. It's unfortunate that the church doesn't always embody love all that well. Sure, there are some people, churches, and movements that embody love really well. But in reality, people are much better at talking about love than living out love. Just about anyone can talk about the importance of love. Just about anyone can say, "I love you." We can all feel love for someone. None of those things make our lives distinct. To truly live a life of love, we must choose to live unselfishly. We must make servanthood a part of our lives. That means that sometimes we don't feel like serving, but we serve anyway. This is a kind of love that must be shaped by God's work inside of us. It is a love that emerges in our lives when we are transformed by the height, the depth, the breadth, and the width of God's love.

Jesus thought it was possible for his followers to embody the same kind of selfless love that he has for us.

Perhaps one of the most significant things that causes us to fall short involves the reality that many professing Christians don't really experience the depths of love that God has for them. We can't love like Jesus in our own strength. It must be formed in us by his transforming work.

We might know and understand that God loves us (in our minds). We may even tell others that God loves them. But how deeply have we experienced the love of God in our hearts? To ignite a movement of love, it must begin in our hearts. We must seek to experience greater depths of God's love in the depths of who we are. It must run deep into our soul. And when it does, transformation will be evident.

In essence, we discover how to love God by realizing that He loves us.

> We love because he first loved us.
>
> *1 John 4:9*

For many years, I knew God's love in my head but not in my heart. In other words, God's love hadn't yet transformed my heart at a deep level. After I spent time studying passages like Ephesians 3:16-19, God began to teach me not just to study the Bible, but to experience the living words of the Bible. He used different people in my life to shed light on this. In light of my experience, would you allow me to guide you into this text? It is a prayer that the Apostle Paul prayed for the Church at Ephesus. I want you to read it a few times. As you do, sink more deeply into experiencing the love of God in your heart.

> I pray that Christ will live in your hearts by faith and that your life will be strong in love and be built on love. And I pray that you and all God's holy people will have the power to understand the greatness of Christ's love – how wide and how long and how high and how deep that love is. Christ's love is greater than anyone can ever know, but I pray that you will be able to know that love. Then you can be filled with the fullness of God.
>
> *Ephesians 3:16-19*

Now, take a few moments to read the excerpt from a talk given by the late Brennan Manning from Live at Woodcrest. His writings have impacted me in my own journey of knowing how to experience God's love personally and deeply for myself.

> The Lord Jesus is going to ask each of us one question and only one question: Did you believe that I loved you? That I desired you? That I waited for you day after day? That I longed to hear the sound of your voice? The real believers there will answer, "Yes, Jesus. I believed in your love and I tried to shape my life as a response to it." But many of us who are so faithful in our ministry, in our practice, in our church going are going to have to reply, "Well frankly, no sir. I mean, I never really believed it. I mean, I heard a lot of wonderful sermons and teachings about it. In fact, I gave quite a few myself. But I always knew that that was just a way of speaking; a kindly lie, some Christian's pious pat on the back to cheer me on." And there's the difference between the real believers and the nominal Christians that are found in our churches across the land. No one can measure like a believer the depth and the intensity of God's love. But at the same time, no one can measure like a believer the effectiveness of our gloom, pessimism, low self-esteem, self-hatred and despair that block God's way to us. Do you see why it is so important to lay hold of this basic truth of our faith? Because you're only going to be as big as your own concept of God.
>
> Do you remember the famous line of the French philosopher, Blaise Pascal? "God made man in his own image, and man returned the compliment?" We often make God in our own image, and He winds up to be as fussy, rude, narrow-minded, legalistic, judgmental, unforgiving, unloving as we are.

Made for More

> In the past couple of three years I have preached the gospel to the financial community in Wall Street, New York City, the airmen and women of the air force academy in Colorado Springs, a thousand positions in Nairobi. I've been in churches in Bangor, Maine, Miami, Chicago, St. Louis, Seattle, San Diego. And honest, the god of so many Christians I meet is a god who is too small for me. Because he is not the God of the Word, he is not the God revealed by it in Jesus Christ who this moment comes right to your seat and says, "I have a word for you. I know your whole life story. I know every skeleton in your closet. I know every moment of sin, shame, dishonesty and degraded love that has darkened your past. Right now I know your shallow faith, your feeble prayer life, your inconsistent discipleship. And my word is this: I dare you to trust that I love you just as you are, and not as you should be. Because you're never going to be as you should be." – Brennan Manning

I do something (almost) every day to center myself in God and remind me of my dependence on him for my worth and identity. It sets the tone for my day when it comes to abiding. Each morning before the chaos, temptations, and earthly dust flies at my face, I close my eyes and say a short prayer: "Lord, you are the one true God. The Father, the Son, and the Holy Spirit. I am your beloved. I will depend on you." I cling to the truth as written in Scripture: "I am my beloved's, and his desire is for me" (Song of Solomon 7:10). As those words float out of my inner being, I take a deep breath. Inhale. Exhale. It's as if God's breath is entering into me as I speak these transcendent words. I find life over and over again in the truth – I am loved by my Father. And that's enough. It has to be. This seems simple, yet it's an unbelievably powerful truth and reality we must remain in touch with if we want to live the lives God created us to live.

The search for who we are, and why we matter, has been with us from the beginning. And it will be with us until the end. As apprentices of Jesus, this search resides inside every person whom God entrusts to our influence. There's only one way to allow God to shape who we are and be reminded of where our worth comes from: that is to attach ourselves to his presence and love every moment we can, like a branch attaching itself to the vine. God is Love. And here's what he's saying to you and to me in every moment of our lives, both now and forever:

You are my son. You are my daughter. You are loved.

WEEK 6
AN UNSTOPPABLE MISSION

Be wise in the way you act toward outsiders; make the most of every opportunity. Let your conversation be always full of grace, seasoned with salt, so that you may know how to answer everyone.
Colossians 4:5-6

6.1 PREPARATION

Thousands of years ago in Roman culture, there was a significant role that a person played. The role was known as a *messenger*. Communication technology wasn't what we have today, so it was necessary to have someone to carry important messages to the people. Depending on the scenario, the role of a messenger would involve waiting for the message that needed to be delivered. For instance, when news was ready to be delivered to the people in town, the messenger took the message to the town square where others in the community typically gathered. That's where the messenger proclaimed the message. Usually, this was a declaration of good news. The message might be about the pregnant queen who just had her baby. The messenger would run to the center of town and proclaim, "The Queen had her baby!" In response, people would celebrate and cheer.

Another example is seen when the messenger waited to hear news about a raging battle that was going on. Upon winning a battle, the commanding officer sent the victorious message with the messenger who would take off running to town to proclaim to the people, "Hail to the victors, we have won the battle! We are victorious!" After hearing the good news, everyone would celebrate.

In those days, people understood the power of good news.

Jettison forward into today's cultural landscape. We hear bad news all the time. The news that gets proclaimed through various media and mediums is typically driven by fears and phobias, insults and lies, stories that revolve around scandals, conspiracy theories, and celebrity gossip. It doesn't take much convincing to say that **our world is desperate for good news.**

Back in the first century, the Apostle Paul wrote a letter to one of his disciples, Timothy. In this letter, he used the Greek word *euangelion,* which means **"someone who brought good news."** He wrote:

> **Do the work of an evangelist (*euangelion*).**
>
> *1 Timothy 4:5*

What comes to your mind when *you* hear the word evangelist?

Typically, when the word evangelist is used, some people get anxious. Others think evangelism is something that certain gifted people do. For many, the word conjures up feelings of guilt because they haven't really done any evangelism. Still, others think about an older man with big and tall bouffant-style, white hair who wants to confront people with a loud, obnoxious, condemning preacher voice. Or maybe that's just me.

Will you put aside any negative connotations that may enter your mind for a minute?

Isn't it interesting that the word evangelist gets used in non-religious contexts (and indeed is used positively)? For example, a friend of mine works at Apple as one of their *chief evangelists.* Literally, that's his official title. His primary role is to be an ambassador for Apple products. I've seen him in action, and he's a great evangelist for Apple products. I've seen him actively and fervently promote a positive message that advocates for Apple products. He's very persuasive simply by his enthusiasm about something that he feels can make a person's life better. In essence, this chief evangelist proclaims *good news* to potential or current customers. He *represents* Apple with passion and purpose. He is a firsthand *witness* as someone who has seen and experienced Apple products. As a result, he shares his distinct and valuable experience with others, in hopes that they will have a similar experience by using the product.

As you know, Apple didn't invent this word. The Apostle Paul didn't either. In fact, Paul co-opted this non-religious, common word from Roman culture. And he used it to communicate something very important about being messengers who carry good news.

Let's go back to 1 Timothy 4:5. Paul says "DO…" That's an action word. The verb tense used in Greek tells the reader that the action never ceases. Paul then continues with the phrase, "do the work of…" What he's saying is, "never cease to take action in bringing the good news to people." The verb choice selected is important because it tells us something about our calling.

Every follower of Jesus must never stop "doing the work of an evangelist." That is, never stop doing the work of someone who brings good news. It's the call of every disciple. It's the ethos of a healthy and vibrant discipleship culture. Unfortunately, most followers of Jesus have stopped doing this evangelistic work. As a result, they've lost sight of a crucial aspect of God's purpose for their life. Recent Barna research reveals that nine out of ten Christians are not comfortable sharing their faith. They aren't actively involved in passing on the good news about the hope we have in Christ.

Proper understanding of 1 Timothy 4:5 spotlights the importance for all disciples to make this task our life's work. This is something Jesus intends for us to do. The Scriptures clearly intend for us to look and pray for opportunities to share the good news with the people in our lives. But that doesn't mean we galavant around telling everyone they are going to hell if they don't believe. It's nothing like that. That's not what Jesus intended or wants from you.

Here's the reality: people are searching for God, and God is calling his disciples to testify about how he is working in their lives, so that others can find what they are searching for.

One of the ways I approach sharing my faith is to pay attention to people who are searching. I listen to what people are saying, but also to the subtext of their conversations. People have longings. They have questions. They wonder about things. And in those moments when something they say or imply has a possible intersection with the Gospel, I lean in. Often, I simply ask more questions and discover that they have real questions about God, faith, and life.

At some point in the conversation, I begin to weave in some of my own story. I do my best to share something with them that might relate to their questions, doubts, or struggles. We all have a testimony worth sharing, but we need to "be wise in the way we act towards outsiders." We need to "make the most of every opportunity." We need to "make our conversations full of grace, seasoned with salt" (see Colossians 4:5-6).

If you've come this far in your reading, chances are you have experienced the Gospel in your life – and it's almost certainly transforming you. One way to think about what you share with others is how God is working in your life. Yes, you have a conversion aspect of your testimony, but sharing the Good News is more than that. The Gospel changes everything about our lives in the here and how, not to mention eternity. Yes, there will be resistance when you share your life and faith with others. But when you share things that you are experiencing now, or have experienced, it's kind of hard for someone to argue with that. You're basically becoming a witness to the work of God.

What if we co-opted this word again? *Euangelion.*

Could it help us return to the core purpose of that word? What if we started to become someone who never stops bringing good news? What if we decided to make this our life's work?

I think we need to reclaim and restore the innocence and beauty of this word. It's *OUR* word anyways… because good news is exactly what the world needs.

In Acts 20:24, we find the anthem of Paul's life:

> …I consider my life worth nothing to me; my only aim is to finish the race and complete the task the Lord Jesus has given me – the task of testifying to the good news of God's grace.

On another occasion, we find Paul articulating his willingness to do anything short of sin to spread the Gospel.

> Now, even though I am free from obligations to others I joyfully make myself a servant to all in order to win as many converts as possible. I became Jewish to the Jewish people in order to win them to the Messiah. I became like one under the law to gain the people who were stuck under the law, even though I myself am not under the law. And to those who are without the Jewish laws, I became like them, as one without the Jewish laws, in order to win them, although I'm not outside the law of God but under

the law of Christ. I became "weak" to the weak to win the weak. I have adapted to the culture of every place I've gone so that I could more easily win people to Christ. I've done all this so that I would become God's partner for the sake of the Gospel.

1 Corinthians 9:19-23

Jesus' passion and heartbeat is to send his disciples into the world to show his love to those who are searching for him. Jesus said, "Just as the father has sent me, now I'm now sending you" (John 20:21).

If you are a devoted Jesus follower, you are called to be a voice of hope and a conduit of God's message of grace and forgiveness.

We have good news. And as disciples and disciple makers, we are called to focus our lives on sharing that with others. We are to make a choice every day to give ourselves away for the sake of blessing, serving, and loving other people. As we give our lives away, not only do we bring God glory, but we discover life as it was meant to be lived. We find our purpose, our divine destiny.

How beautiful on the mountains are the feet of the messenger who brings good news, the good news of peace and salvation, the news that the God of Israel reigns!

Isaiah 52:7

6.2 STUDY

In the early church narrative of Acts, we find a woman named Lydia who lived on mission with passionate focus. She was an audacious ambassador for Christ who refused to let fear, distraction, or anything else hinder her missional impact on people. Her life is an inspiring story of a courageous representative of Jesus Christ. Her life is a living witness of the power of the Gospel.

Lydia came to faith through the ministry of Paul. She was discipled by Paul, and then became a disciple maker herself. God later used her to plant the first church in Philippi.

> On the Sabbath we went outside the city gate to the river, where we expected to find a place of prayer. We sat down and began to speak to the women who had gathered there. One of those listening was a woman from the city of Thyatira named Lydia, a dealer in purple cloth. She was a worshiper of God. The Lord opened her heart to respond to Paul's message. When she and the members of her household were baptized, she invited us to her home. "If you consider me a believer in the Lord," she said, "come and stay at my house." And she persuaded us.
>
> *Acts 16:13-15*

We discover some interesting details about Lydia's personal and professional life that give us context and insight about how to live on mission. First, Lydia had an eye for design and a knack for making money. She was much like a fashion CEO in our day. Her primary product was purple cloth, which was the color of royalty (purple was an expensive dye). Lydia was also an entrepreneur and a successful businesswoman in a culture that didn't value women.

Lydia was originally from a city called Thyatira but moved to Philippi, likely because this was the most prominent city in the district of Macedonia (modern day Greece). There weren't many places for people to buy, sell, and trade quite like Philippi. In that regard, Lydia remained intentional and strategic with the gifts and abilities God had given her. She was a good steward of the resources that she'd been blessed with, as we all should be.

In addition, Lydia was the first disciple in Europe. And since she had become a successful leader, a wealthy woman, and now a person of faith, there was great potential to reach her unique circles of influence, especially in the city of Philippi (her primary residence). This city was larger than most, so it became a significant part of her expanding ministry.

Lydia's home eventually became the gathering place of the first church planted in Europe (Philippi). What started in ordinary conversations among a few people eventually catapulted into a church plant that had a significant impact on Lydia's circle of influence. As her story evolved, Lydia's influence became exponential through her relationships with fellow Christ followers. She partnered with others to reach people who were not being reached. And in the midst of persecution and resistance, these disciples took initiative, faced their fears, and risked their lives to jettison the Gospel message throughout the world. Through ordinary yet courageous conversations, the Good News was shared freely. This fueled the movement of God in the first century, leaving a ripple effect throughout Europe.

Lydia lived boldly and proactively. She spoke up as Christ's **resilient representative** to people in her circles of influence and impacted her community by doing things no one else was doing. She was a **kingdom entrepreneur** and **audacious Gospel ambassador** for Christ.

Lydia used the resources God gave her to serve people who didn't yet know God. She was **generous, hospitable**, and **intentional**.

Lydia **took initiative** and **seized opportunities** to share Christ with people in her life. She was a **radical risk-taker** and **courageous conversation starter**. As a result, Lydia's impact was far more expansive than she ever imagined.

Living like Lydia is uncommon. But her counter-cultural, Gospel-centered life is inspiring. In our day, who do you know that lives like Lydia? Can you imagine if our churches were filled with people who embodied her spirit and essence? What if disciples everywhere took radical risks for the Gospel, built intentional relationships with people who were far from God, and used their resources to bless others with generosity and hospitality?

Imagine if Christ followers everywhere were constantly speaking up with boldness, courage, and humility as they spread the Good News.

What if every follower of Jesus figured out ways to partner with others to reach people who aren't being reached by doing things that weren't being done? What if *you* could discover how to become a Gospel ambassador like Lydia, and as a result, see your influence expand in a far more expansive way than you can even imagine?

> How can they call on him to save them unless they believe in him? And how can they believe in him if they have never heard about him? And how can they hear about him unless someone tells them?
>
> *Romans 1:14*
>
> We are ambassadors of the Anointed One who carry the message of Christ to the world, as though God were tenderly pleading with them directly through our lips. So we tenderly plead with you on Christ's behalf, "Turn back to God and be reconciled to him."
>
> *1 Corinthians 5:20*
>
> …pray for me that when I speak, God will give me words so that I can tell the secret of the Good News without fear. I have been sent to preach this Good News, and I am doing that now, here in prison. Pray that when I preach the Good News I will speak without fear, as I should.
>
> *Ephesians 6:19-20*

Self-Reflection

Why do you think that the vast majority of professing Christians stay on the sidelines? Why do they remain passive in sharing their faith? And if they aren't sharing their faith in some way, do you ever wonder how deeply the Gospel has really pervaded their hearts? I do.

Though there are many obstacles, I believe that many either lack passion for God or lack a personal and authentic connection with God. On top of that, they have a fear of rejection. Some have a weak faith, feel inadequate to share their faith, or maintain self-doubt. Also, the Enemy persistently tries to derail us, tempt us, lie to us, and altogether stop us from advancing the message of the Gospel. And then, he tries to throw shame and accusations our way. Basically, he does anything he can to deceive, distract, and derail us in hopes that he will hinder God's message and purpose from advancing.

Needless to say, it's no small task to stay aligned with God and engaged with his mission. And trust me, I can relate to the struggles and challenges, the fears and self-doubt, and even to the fear of rejection. That's why I often remind myself of this reality. I make a mindful choice to do my part when it comes to reaching out to people who are far from God – remembering that God promises to do his part. One of the ways I try to reach my friends is by playing golf with them regularly, going to lunch or dinner with people who don't know or follow God, and simply by showing kindness to people in my neighborhood, when I am shopping, at a restaurant, or sitting at a coffee shop. On my best days, I pray for opportunities to share my faith and be a voice of hope and encouragement to someone with the Gospel. I try to bless people in some way, and look for opportunities to engage a meaningful conversation.

All that being said, I'm human just like you. And that means that my passion and urgency ebb and flow – maybe yours does too. I have moments that I miss. I have opportunities that I don't make the most of. I walk away from people sometimes having failed to share my faith, or feeling like I said the wrong thing. But, I do my best to remain grateful to God for opportunities to learn and engage in spiritual conversations. And God continues to remind me of his grace, of what he's done for me, and of what he offers to all humanity.

What is your current level of **passion** and **urgency** to live out God's mission?

1	2	3	4	5	6	7	8	9	10
Mild				*Medium*					*Hot*

Specifically, what hinders you from bearing witness to the Gospel or from sharing your faith story with others? We all have some obstacles, so what are yours? Identify two or three challenges/obstacles that you need to face personally when it comes to sharing the Gospel and living on mission. Jot down a few things that hinder you from sharing your faith (i.e. lack of passion or connection with God, fear of rejection, inadequacy, self-doubt, anxiety, lack of knowledge, lack of faith, mission just isn't a priority, don't know people who aren't yet following Jesus, etc.).

CHANGE

There are three identities that we take on that fuel our pursuit of missional living:

1. **You are an AMBASSADOR of Christ.**

    Ambassador: to act as a **representative** (of Latin origin, meaning servant or minister).

    We are **ambassadors,** speaking on behalf of the Messiah, as though God were making his appeal through us.
    1 Corinthians 5:20

    To be an **ambassador** of Christ means that we are diplomatic agents (sent and authorized by King Jesus) to speak on his behalf.

    We represent him.

    We are the voice of heaven to the earth.

    We are servants of King Jesus, infused with power from the Holy Spirit and by the authority of Christ's blood.

2. **You are a WITNESS of the Gospel.**

   Witness: used to describe an action and a person; someone who sees or hears something, then talks about what they saw or heard.

   > ...you will receive power when the Holy Spirit comes upon you. And you will be my **witnesses, telling people about me everywhere – in Jerusalem, throughout Judea, in Samaria, and to the ends of the earth.**
   >
   > *Acts 1:8 NLT*

   The term witness often makes us think of someone who testifies in front of judges, usually in a courtroom context. But to be a **witness** simply means that we see or hear something significant. Then, we share what we saw. If a witness shares what they see or hear, they are *bearing witness.* God desires for his followers to see him and hear him – and then represent him to the world.

   One of the primary roles of God's people throughout Scripture is to bear witness. God desires to have a tribe of witnesses who have seen him and experienced him. He wants that tribe to represent him to the world by bearing witness to the God they have encountered and know personally and intimately.

   Throughout the Scriptures, God usually appoints a chief witness to help his people represent him well. In the Old Testament, for example, he does so in Exodus,

Deuteronomy, and Isaiah. In the New Testament, Jesus is the *Chief Witness* (or Representative) who offers rescue, freedom, and salvation. Notice that Jesus claims the title of "Witness" on several occasions (see John 8:14, 17-18). He is the Supreme Witness who declares who he is and proclaims that God's kingdom has come through him. Throughout the gospels, a plethora of people witness his works and his words. Many people respond to his message, while other people reject the testimony they hear. In the end, some who refused to believe end up killing him for what they wrongly accused him of: bearing false witness.

Ultimately, the *Chief Witness* provides hope for all creation to be restored through the cross and resurrection. And as the biblical narrative unfolds, Jesus sends out his followers as his witnesses who proclaim the kingdom of God and offer hope and restoration to a world in need. At one point, he tells his disciples, "As the Father has sent me, so I am sending you" (John 20:21).

For a person who hears the story of God and experiences the love of God, the most natural thing to do is share the Good News with others.

3. **You are a WORSHIPER of God.**

    Cultivating a missional heart always flows from living a worshipful life.

> Beloved friends, what should be our proper response to God's marvelous mercies? I encourage you to surrender yourselves to God to be his sacred, living sacrifices. And live in holiness, experiencing all that delights his heart. For this becomes your **genuine expression of worship**. Stop imitating the ideals and opinions of the culture around you, but be inwardly transformed by the Holy Spirit through a total reformation of how you think. This will empower you to discern God's will as you live a beautiful life, satisfying and perfect in his eyes.
>
> *Romans 12:1-2*

To align our hearts on mission, we must align our hearts in worship. These are two inseparable realities. As we worship God in our day-to-day lives, we cultivate deeper connection and increased awareness of who God is and what he's doing in the world. We begin to focus more on him, and less on ourselves. He increases and we decrease. The embers of our hearts' affections get kindled when we worship God. Our compassion deepens when we experience his abounding love and we become motivated to participate in bringing restoration and renewal to God's creation.

Worshiping God is not simply about singing songs to him, though I often connect deeply with God through those experiences. According to God, our worship is how we live every day of our lives: how we relate to others, how we approach work, how we manage our finances, and how we steward our gifts and talents.

Our quest to live on mission comes alive when we connect our hearts to God.

Then, our desire for God's will grows and deepens. We begin to reflect who we worship. We become conduits of God's love in this world – and we suddenly become the proof of God's love to those around us. Our missional lifestyle and heartbeat become part of who we are and become evident in how we live. And when that reality exists in and through our lives, our impact in this world begins to spread and influence people on a personal level. We begin to become people who aren't focused on ourselves but on others. And it's inspiring to those around us.

What does it look like to be a disciple who shares his/her faith? Well, as we continue to fix our eyes and hearts on Jesus, the Gospel pervades every aspect of our lives. As a result of our new Gospel identity, we find ourselves doing what Jesus would be doing, saying what he would be saying, and feeling what he would be feeling. Even more specifically, we relate to those outside the family of God in ways that resemble how Jesus related to those on the outside. Namely, with compassion, love, grace, and radical inclusivity. We start to pray compassionate prayers like Jesus would pray – with urgency and faith. We also begin to speak with increased authority and boldness as well as the fruit of humility and gentleness that comes from the indwelling Holy Spirit. We become people who are prepared to tell others about the hope that we have in Christ (i.e. we bear witness). We do all this with wisdom and grace as well as gentleness and respect – just like Christ would if he were in our place (1 Peter 3:15; 1 John 2:6). We become wise in the way we act towards outsiders and make the most of every opportunity (Colossians 4:5-6). We become a voice of hope to those we interact with. You could say we become *hope carriers.* In essence, we continue to embody God's heart and mission as we strive to partner with him, who "...wants all people to be saved and come to a knowledge of the truth" (1 Timothy 2:4).

6.4 ACTION

Several years ago, there was a college student (I'll call her Emily) who started attending our church. Within a few months, she started to follow Jesus. In one of our conversations, Emily told me that she wasn't an "evangelist." Then she said, "...and I'll never become one either." In response, I wanted to understand what she meant and why she said that. So I asked some questions. Turns out, she was (by her own admission) very timid when it came to discussing spiritual matters with people who didn't believe in God. She had seen people force their beliefs on others, including herself, and that turned her off to evangelism for years. As a result, she was declaring that she wouldn't be like that now that she was a Jesus follower. Emily also told me, "I'm just not a confrontational person," and "I don't think it's my calling to convert people." She had become a worshiper, but not yet an ambassador or witness. These were some of her mental obstacles to becoming a witness of the Gospel and an ambassador for Christ.

Emily was new on her spiritual journey, so I wanted to approach this situation thoughtfully and respectfully. But I also wanted to challenge her thinking, and potentially help her rethink what it meant to share Christ with others in her circles of influence. My goal was to help her reframe what this meant for her life as a disciple. I wanted to remind her of her calling and God's greater purpose.

As we talked, I paid attention to what she liked to do for fun (her hobbies, passions, and interests). There are often natural points of relational connection in environments that we already enjoy being in that can lead to deeper friendships and conversations.

At some point, these can be the bridges that we build to help others find and follow Christ.

Two of Emily's interests that jumped out to me were her cooking skills and passion to host. More specifically, she mentioned how much she loved making fondue, which led me to think, "What if I helped Emily throw fondue parties for her friends as a way to build bridges to the Gospel?" She loved the idea!

After pulling together a small team, we cast the vision, and offered a few helpful guidelines. Then off we went. We reminded everyone to be intentional in conversations, but that the goal was to build relationships and pay attention to any opportunities to talk about God that arose. We weren't going to force anything – that never works out anyway. Instead, we would build genuine relationships, ask lots of questions, care about people, serve people, and even pray for those who might come.

The fondue party was a relational-focused event that created a non-threatening environment for people who weren't quite ready to follow Christ.

We began throwing these parties monthly at her modest, but very trendy 800-square-foot studio apartment. At the third party, we had over eighty people! That became the norm month after month. Then, in natural conversations, we eventually invited some people to our church, which happened to gather in a nightclub on Sunday nights just down the road. To our delight, a number of people visited our church. And weeks and months later, some of them eventually put their faith in Christ!

There are many incredible faith stories that I could share, but here's my main point: Emily's viewpoint about "how to live on mission" was radically realigned. In fact, this whole experience became a defining season of her life, as she discovered how to live on mission in a way that was unique to her. I remember when she thanked me for believing in her as well as helping her discover what she referred to as "a way to do evangelism that just feels like me."

Let this be a reminder about how overwhelming evangelism can seem, yet how simple things like hospitality, hobbies, and natural friendships can help make an eternal impact a real possibility. Don't buy into the belief that you need a large and established platform to be effective at reaching people who don't yet know God. You can do this in your everyday, ordinary life.

There are many dimensions to living on mission with God, and sometimes we make it more complicated than it needs to be.

Maybe you consider yourself a non-evangelist like Emily. It's not true. Evangelism has always been about sharing the Good News. It's about realizing that the Gospel has transformed your life, and then making a decision to share that Gospel with others in ways that honor them, include them, and show them respect for the journey they are on. Sharing one's faith has never been something that was intended only for certain gifted people. And it may never happen without some internal fear and anxiety. So if you're a disciple of Jesus, you just may need to discover ways to bear witness that fit who we are and how you uniquely relate to others.

Again, Emily didn't think of herself as an evangelist – far from it. But she became a person, much like Lydia, who had an impact on her circles of influence in ways she never imagined. Emily learned how to become a representative of Christ and a witness of the Gospel. She became a Gospel ambassador who sparked a new initiative by using her time, talents, and treasures to serve others. Just like us, she had self-doubt, fears, and some misguided thinking. But deep down, she wanted to make an impact – she just didn't know how. And since her heart was in the right place, she remained open to new possibilities. As a result, she was encouraged by a fellow disciple and inspired to take action in unique ways. She ended up reaching people who weren't being reached because she cared enough to do something that wasn't being done.

Is there any risk or new endeavor that God is prompting you to take on?

Are you prepared to listen to the voice of the Holy Spirit, and allow him to lead you into taking new kinds of risks to advance the Gospel for the sake of others?

> Our lives are a Christ-like fragrance rising up to God. But this fragrance is perceived differently by those who are being saved and by those who are perishing. To those who are perishing, we are a dreadful smell of death and doom. But to those who are being saved, we are a life-giving perfume. And who is adequate for such a task as this? You see, we are not like the many hucksters who preach for personal profit. We preach the word of God with sincerity and with Christ's authority, knowing that God is watching us.
>
> *2 Corinthians 2:15-17*

And please pray for me, that God will open a door of opportunity for us to preach the revelation of the mystery of Christ, for whose sake I am imprisoned. Pray that I would unfold and reveal fully this mystery, for that is my delightful assignment. Walk in the wisdom of God as you live before the unbelievers, and make it your duty to make him known. Let every word you speak be drenched with grace and tempered with truth and clarity. For then you will be prepared to give a respectful answer to anyone who asks about your faith.

Colossians 4:3-6

But give reverent honor in your hearts to the Anointed One and treat him as the holy Master of your lives. And if anyone asks about the hope living within you, always be ready to explain your faith.

1 Peter 3:15

Yes, we will follow your ways, Lord Yahweh, and entwine our hearts with yours, for the fame of your name is all that we desire.

Isaiah 26:8

6.5 COMMUNITY

SPARK: Any small, controllable risk that is intended to inspire or otherwise improve the individual or the world around him.

Disciples are called to be a **spark** of God's mission in the world as we strive to restore what has been damaged.

After adequate time socializing and eating a meal together, it's time to facilitate what we will call a Spark Group experience. This is an idea that my friend Jason introduced to me years ago. This is going to involve serving our friends and neighbors who aren't yet following Jesus. We're going to identify one risk to take that you believe can spark intentionality and missional living. To become a Gospel ambassador, you have to be proactive, remain willing to take risks, embody courage and faith, and live with intentionality. You can do this. To be missional requires that you identify others' interests and needs so that you can uniquely and creatively serve them and meet their needs – relationally, physically, emotionally, spiritually, etc. Again, you can do this!

Discussion: As a group, take a few moments to think about a risk you could take that would serve someone in your life that doesn't yet follow God. Our goal is to *spark* something in you tonight (and in others this week). It could involve something as simple as initiating a meet up with a friend who you haven't spent time with lately in an effort to reignite your friendship. It could involve inviting a friend to church or asking someone questions about their spiritual journey. Maybe you feel a bit intimidated to ask, but for you, it's something you know you need to do. It could involve serving someone in your neighborhood who is in need, organizing an event, or hosting something at your home. It could involve volunteering or giving to an organization that you've been wanting to serve alongside. There really aren't any right or wrong answers, as long as you focus on serving and loving someone who isn't yet following Jesus. You're focused on doing good, and bringing good news to people. The prayer is that, with God's help, this discussion will spark something,

Next week, we will come back together to share how it all went. This is a form of accountability.

Directions: Once you decide what risk you will take to spark good in your world, take time in group discussion for each person to share what they plan to do. Focus on one person at a time. Give time for the person to elaborate on why the risk they are going to take is important to them. Once the idea is shared, the group is free to ask questions, probe deeper, and dialogue to gain a better understanding. Once the person has shared adequately, go on to the next person. Make sure someone records everyone's "risk" for next week when the group meets again to discuss how things went.

For next week: Prepare to discuss how things went (good or bad, success or failure), what happened, what was hard, what was the outcome, where you saw God at work, or why you backed out of it. Come back to share with one another. Then, bring another risk that you'll take the week after that. If the group chooses, keep this going for a few weeks and see how God works. Going forward, the hope is that you will make risk-taking a part of your life as a disciple.

FOCUS

Jesus called himself the light of the world (John 8:12). What made him shine? Sometimes, it was his words (John 7:46). But it wasn't only his words – it was also his works. He said, "The works that I do in my Father's name bear witness about me" (John 10:25). Jesus' works revealed who he was and what he valued. His works shined then, and now, our works can still shine. Ultimately, they are to shine with his glory, not our own.

Jesus called us the light of the world:

> You are the light of the world. A city set on a hill cannot be hidden. Nor do people light a lamp and put it under a basket, but on a stand, and it gives light to all in the house. In the same way, let your light shine before others, so that they may see your good works and give glory to your Father who is in heaven.
>
> *Matthew 5:14-16*

What makes us shine? It isn't only our words. It is also our works.

> Preach the gospel at all times, and if necessary use words. – St. Francis of Assisi

The works we do in Jesus' name bear witness about us and about him. Our outward, observable good deeds (or works) make who we are (and whose we are) manifestly clear. Just like Jesus, our works cause some to revile us, persecute us, and utter all kinds of evil against us. And our good deeds cause others to give glory to our heavenly Father.

Jesus declared, "A city set on a hill cannot be hidden" (Matthew 5:14).

What kind of good works shine like that? Ask yourself, what good works have other Christians done that stand out most in your memory? Who are the people you've known who have been most radiant with the light of Jesus?

The people who shine aren't necessarily the smartest or most articulate. They aren't necessarily the most talented, nor do they need to have the most publicly influential platforms. Usually, they've been the most servant-hearted and sacrificially loving. They've been the ones who find God's steadfast love better than life (Psalm 63:3). They've consistently loved others in both word and deed (1 John 3:18). Their words and deeds have sometimes been tender and other times tough, depending on the need of the moment. Their actions have demonstrated that they truly consider others more significant than themselves, and that they pursue others' good more than others' approval (Philippians 2:3).

What makes these shining people remarkable is not only *what* they do, it's *why* and *how* they do it. When we do good perpetually and serve others consistently, people are impacted. It is our *doing* more than anything, not our talking, that sets us apart and expands our impact. We find ourselves drawn to people who truly "live it" because the light of their humble, word-and-deed love has both warmed our chilled hearts and exposed our selfishness and pride.

Disciples ought to be people who constantly, consistently, and abundantly *do good*. Doing good often involves meeting people's physical, relational, spiritual, or emotional needs. So, if you want to be an "evangelist," perhaps some of you need to simply start meeting other people's real-life needs. Bring them that *good news*.

> **Whenever you possibly can, do good to those who need it. Never tell your neighbors to wait until tomorrow if you can help them now.**
> *Proverbs 3:27-28*
>
> **Whenever we have the opportunity, we should do good to everyone.**
> *Galatians 6:10*

Over the years, many people have helped shape who I've become. They have discipled me. And, God has also placed people in my life that I've been fortunate to have the opportunity to disciple. Some of the people I've discipled ended up teaching and inspiring me. These disciples took their calling seriously. They leveraged their unique passions, gifting, and creativity to reach others. These friends didn't just proclaim the Good News with their words – they lived out the Good News in their lives. They each recognized that the Gospel can be shared by how we live, not just by what we say.

Hope Carriers

Here are a few brief stories that can spur you on to do good in the world, bring Good News, and meet people's needs with the life-giving Gospel that bears fruit through your life. These are friends of mine who carried hope to people who needed it. They took on a different perspective, and began to see their family, work, school, and everyday life as a mission. Living on mission can seem overwhelming at times, and as a result, leave you not knowing where to start. These stories give some insight into how you can take initiative in your own life as you strive to become a hope carrier and Gospel ambassador.

Michael lived as a Gospel ambassador and hope carrier who had a heart for getting clean water to desperate places. As a result, he decided to fund and build a well in Ghana. He did all the research necessary and then organized a plan that invited twenty-five people to give $10 a week for three months (equaling $3,000, the cost for a well). He set it up online and took initiative to bring good news to people by meeting a physical need, with hopes of meeting a spiritual need. It took courage and faith. He leveraged his relationships to do something really good. Fast forward three years. Michael ended up raising funds to build more than 250 wells and eight cisterns in seventeen countries that served over 100,000 people with clean, safe drinking water. And by the way, Michael involved non-believing people in this journey to build wells, which was an amazing example to them of what a Christ follower can and should be all about. He was an *evangelion* who shared the Gospel in multi-dimensional ways. He propelled the Gospel by living out the Gospel.

Justin, Jonathan, and Joe were all Gospel ambassadors and hope carriers who decided to bring Good News in the form of starting a grass-roots mentoring program at a public junior high school in Los Angeles. It wasn't a "Christian-based" school, but over time, their ministry became a portal of Christ-centered influence to these young students, their families and even a few teachers. This took courage and faith. It also took a willingness to fail. These three young men took initiative to make an impact right where they were living. Through the relationships that they built, the Gospel advanced in actions and later in words. And what followed was transformation – in their lives and in the lives of others. They were embodying what it means to be an empowered disciple who is striving to make other disciples.

David and Brittany wanted to bring Good News to the creative community in Los Angeles. So they started a monthly event for twenty-something artists. They leveraged the artistic talents of the people they knew (or whom others in their church knew). They designed a monthly event where artists, photographers, filmmakers, musicians, poets, writers, and others could display their work. They came up with themes that were positive, and used the night to build relationships and do good in their city. In that context, they sought to be witnesses and representatives of Christ. The focus was relational. The spiritual texture that they created was central. As a result of their intentionality, frequent spiritual conversations emerged, and people were intrigued by this way of sharing the Gospel. In response, the artists would often donate their work to good causes, which fostered other spiritual conversations. There were many people who David and Brittany met along the way who were searching for God. People would often ask questions about why they were doing what they were doing. In natural ways, they talked about the importance of God in their lives. Mostly, they focused on serving people's needs and being a voice of hope to them.

Each of these people embodied urgency about the mission. They had a heart to connect with those who were searching for God and in desperate need of hope and Gospel-transformation. These friends of mine seized opportunities with courage, faith, creativity, and initiative. They brought the Good News to people in need, in many different forms. They met people's needs and paid attention to their interests, thoughtfully building bridges to the Gospel. This is what it looks like to be a disciple in real life and make other disciples. You encourage and you serve. You think creatively and are proactive. You offer hope. You bless people in ordinary moments and in ordinary ways. When we do this as disciples in churches across the globe, we will discover the impact that cultivating a discipleship culture can bring!

> Whoever watches the wind will not plant; whoever looks at the clouds will not reap. As you do not know the path of the wind, or how the body is formed in a mother's womb, so you cannot understand the work of God, the Maker of all things. Sow your seed in the morning, and at evening let your hands not be idle, for you do not know which will succeed, whether this or that, or whether both will do equally well.
>
> *Ecclesiastes 11:4-6*

In your context, how can you serve and love people who don't yet follow Jesus? How can you bring hope to people in your everyday life?

> Now may God, the fountain of Hope, fill you to overflowing with uncontainable joy and perfect peace as you trust in him. And may the power of the Holy Spirit continually surround your life with his super-abundance until you radiate with hope.
>
> *Romans 15:13*

6.7 REST

Today, I want you to read the verse below and really sit with it. Too often, we are always striving, doing, and trying to produce something. I'm as guilty as anyone. But sometimes, the best thing we can do is be still and realize who God is and ponder what he thinks about us. He takes great delight in YOU. He sings songs of joy over YOU. When he thinks about YOU, he smiles with a full heart of gladness and love. And it's a powerful thing to center ourselves in our Gospel identity, an identity that reminds us how God feels about us.

> For the LORD your God is living among you. He is a mighty savior. He will take delight in you with gladness. With his love, he will calm all your fears. He will rejoice over you with joyful songs.
>
> *Zephaniah 3:17*

God really does delight in you! He created you, and wants to be with you. He also wants you to know how he feels about you, and to savor that every day of your life. May rest remain part of your life rhythm for the rest of your life! May it recharge you, revive you, re-energize you, and restore you. Along the way, I pray that God teaches you how to trust him when you're resting, remembering that God is for you. He sees you and hears you. God is not only the Creator of the Universe, he's the Sustainer of all things. He's your Provider, your Shepherd, your Comforter, your Guide, your Healer, your Friend, your Lord, your Forgiver, your Leader… and he's so much more. So continue to live each day knowing who God is, and how he views and values you. And then, seek to know him and live out of your identity in him. Most of all, remind yourself daily that you are loved by God! Deeply. Profoundly. Personally. Eternally.

As you read these verses, I pray that you would encounter the love of God in a deep way.

> So I kneel humbly in awe before the Father of our Lord Jesus, the Messiah, the perfect Father of every father and child in heaven and on the earth. And I pray that he would unveil within you the unlimited riches of his glory and favor until supernatural strength floods your innermost being with his divine might and explosive power. Then, by constantly using your faith, the life of Christ will be released deep inside you, and the resting place of his love will become the very source and root of your life. Then you will be empowered to discover what every holy one experiences – the great magnitude of the astonishing love of Christ in all its dimensions. How deeply intimate and far-reaching is his love! How enduring and inclusive it is! Endless love beyond measurement that transcends our understanding – this extravagant love pours into you until you are filled to overflowing with the fullness of God! *Never doubt* God's mighty power to work in you and accomplish all this. He will achieve infinitely more than your greatest request, your most unbelievable dream, and exceed your wildest imagination! He will outdo them all, for his miraculous power constantly energizes you.
>
> *Ephesians 3:14-20*

CONCLUSION

AN UNSCRIPTED FUTURE

Your future cannot be predicted or known. But that seems to be how God wants it. And when we look at the Scriptures, we discover that God invites us to walk with him every step of the way, learning how to trust him no matter what we face or where we end up. Along the way, we have defining moments where God changes us or shifts where our lives are headed. God also brings instrumental people into our lives to teach us lessons or give us the wisdom we need for the current season. This is all part of God's plan for your life. It's a future that doesn't have a script, one that requires a growing trust and courageous faith to do the next right thing we know to do. And we're reminded that our journey unfolds day by day, and that we are called to make the most of every day.

There's a story of a young man named Cassius Clay, better known as Muhammad Ali. His famous fighting style was, "Float like a butterfly and sting like a bee." He told a story from when he was just twelve years old and had a bike stolen by another boy in the neighborhood. He wanted to get revenge – to "whup the boy," as he said in an interview. However, he received some advice from a local police officer. In essence he said, "Before you go fight that boy, you should learn how to box." So, Ali did just that. But here's the deal: instead of using his new skills to beat up that boy, Cassius realized that he was *made for more*.

Several weeks later, he had his first boxing match. And he won. And then he won again. And again. By 1964, he was the heavyweight champion of the world and is now heralded as the greatest boxer to have ever lived.

Muhammad Ali recognized that he was made for more than just beating up someone who wronged him. During his career, he was fond of saying "Don't count the days. Make the days count." Although he wasn't quoting the Scriptures, this is the message that the Scriptures pass on to us:

Made for More

> Teach us to number our days and recognize how few they are; help us to spend them as we should.
> *Psalm 90:12*

I want to encourage you with these words: **make the days count.**

Sometimes, life beats you up and you want revenge. But you were made for more than just responding to how life treats you. This season of life may look and feel different than you thought – and that may be uncomfortable, uncertain, or unsettling. But if you will remember that you were made for more, God will transform you into something – or someone – far beyond what you can imagine!

You have a divine destiny.

You have a unique purpose.

You have a special calling from God.

If you will align your life with Jesus by submitting yourself to his will every day, and if you will abide in Christ and his love every day, you will begin to discover God's dreams and designs for your one and only life! Yes, the future is uncertain. And yes, sometimes life can be unsettling or uncomfortable. But as you move through your life, remember that you will never be on the losing side because victory is already yours in Christ Jesus! God wants to be in an ongoing relationship with you, and along the way, he wants to guide you, strengthen you, and transform you. So go live out your calling every day, centering your life in the Gospel, and living a Gospel-centered life. After all, that is who God made you to be, and how he created you to live! You are called to BE a disciple... and you are also called to MAKE disciples.

> I urge you to live a life worthy of the calling you have received.
>
> *Ephesians 4:1*

Acknowledgements

We want to say thank you to a few people who contributed to this book in unique ways. To some of our friends who gave input and insight: Dave Willis, Jeremy McCarter, Chad Lunsford, Michael Steiner, Melanie Sprouse, and Dana Davis. To Abbey Tregglehudder for your investment of time with your editing that made this book way better for the reader! To Ray Vander Laan whose theological work shaped our discipleship journey many years ago and still lives on. To Steve and Carrie McCoy who inspired us to write about discipleship. And to our wives Karen Ingle and Cheri Saccone, who always provide incredible support, encouragement, and insight in our own journey of life and discipleship.

Here are few recommended resources:

- Discipleship resources published by Missio Publishing: *Transformed, The Gospel Primer, Bigger Gospel, The Tangible Kingdom Primer, The Justice Primer, The Permanent Revolution Playbook.* You can also go to **missiopublishing.com** for more information or to place an order.

- Books by Kent Ingle: *Framework Leadership, The Modern Guide to College, The Adventure Called Life, 9 Disciplines of Enduring Leadership.*

- Books by Steve Saccone: *Relational Intelligence, Protege, Talking About God.*

- Download the Amazing Discipleship App called **Small Circle**. It's free and has rich content for being a disciple and making disciples.